THE REUNION

THE REUNION

HAROLD G. SPEER, JR.

ISBN Hardcover: 979-8-9929902-0-1
ISBN eBook: 979-8-9929902-1-8

Interior Design: Creative Publishing Book Design

Dedicated to Grace

TABLE OF CONTENTS

CRETE

SOLVING THE MURDER

ACKNOWLEDGMENT

I want to thank my wife Grace for her constant inspiration and assistance. Without her insightful guidance and her travel companionship, I would never have completed this book. I also thank my sister-in-law Chrissie Allen and my daughter Zoe Speer for their excellent editorial suggestions. Finally, I thank Richard Bomar and Kay Wiles for acting as my sounding board.

PROLOGUE

CHAPTER 1

THE FUNERAL

It was a hot, muggy Saturday afternoon when my wife, Gillian Stuart, and I pulled into the Cedar Bluff Presbyterian Church parking lot in West Knoxville. I found a parking spot among the many cars already on the lot. "Connor," Gillian said, "Look, there is the Hearse parked near the entrance." It was the second time in a week that Gillian and I had made the drive to Knoxville from our home in East Nashville. The first trip had started as a happy and exciting occasion when Gillian and I had traveled to Knoxville to attend my 50th High School reunion last Thursday.

Everything had gone great at the Reunion until the final few minutes of the Saturday night dinner, when to everyone's shock and dismay, Steve Sanders, my popular classmate, collapsed on the floor from what appeared to be a heart attack. He was rushed to the hospital where he was pronounced dead. It was Steve's funeral that had brought Gillian and me back to Knoxville today.

Steve was one of the best basketball players and top scorers in the city during my high school days. He was such a pleasure to watch! He reminded me of Larry Bird. Our Senior Class voted him "Most

Athletic" superlative. He was tall and had frizzy brown hair. He and his older sister, Susan, lived up the street from me. I first met Steve when he played on my Little League football team.

When Steve was not on the basketball court, his high energy level continued and frequently found an outlet through mischievous actions. He was always thinking up crazy things to do, then convincing others to join him. The stories of his escapades with classmates are legendary. So, understandably, my classmates and I were visibly upset when he collapsed at our reunion.

Gillian and I made our way into the church. I was dressed in my black suit and Gillian wore a black dress and black hat. We managed to find seats near the front where we could see the closed casket beside a big picture of Steve on an easel. Seated in the front row with Steve's widow, Sherry, were his sister Susan, and his mother. They were all dressed in black and were periodically wiping their tears away with handkerchiefs they held in their hands. Susan had her arm around Sherry. Steve's father passed away about five years ago. There must have been at least a hundred people in the church pews, including many of my classmates.

Sherry had been the head cheerleader at West High and had dated Steve off and on while they were at West High. She then followed him to East Tennessee State University in Johnson City, where they got married in the summer after their junior year. I knew Sherry well and had dated her for a time during my sophomore year at West. She had kept her cheerleader figure and looked younger than she was.

Several of my classmates were sitting in the pews next to me — Blake, Rusty, Sandy, Henry, Mimi, Bill, Beverly, Pam, Donnie, LeeAnn, and John. Everyone nodded their heads and then directed their eyes to the front of the church, where Preacher McMillan stood up to begin the service.

"Today is a very sad day for the friends and loved ones of Steve Sanders," Preacher McMillan began. I looked around and saw all the solemn faces and I knew that my classmates felt as bad as I did about losing one of our special friends. Steve was so full of life, and it was hard to believe that he would no longer be around. His death was strange, I thought. He looked as if he was still in good shape, and he didn't smoke. Given that his mother was still alive, and his father had lived to age 87, a heart attack at age 68 seemed a little premature for Steve.

Preacher McMillan developed his sermon around Psalms 34:18 - "The Lord is close to the brokenhearted; he rescues those whose spirits are crushed." When he had finished, Susan walked to the front and gave a short eulogy, mentioning what a close bond her family and Steve's classmates had with Steve and how greatly he would be missed. Preacher McMillan closed with a prayer and gave instructions on how to get to the Cedar Bluff Cemetery.

Everyone stood and the eight pallbearers, which included several of Steve's former basketball teammates, carried the casket down the aisle to the waiting hearse outside. Gillian and I followed the crowd out of the church, where we returned to our car and followed the line of cars to the cemetery.

We arrived at the large cemetery, which was attractive, insofar as cemeteries can be. The many tombstones were set among the sprawling and rolling green landscape that was expertly manicured and broken by the occasional shady tree. The sun shone down on the brightly colored flowers that adorned most of the tombstones. Gillian and I followed the group to Steve's waiting plot where the casket was sitting beside the freshly dug six-foot hole and the pile of dirt next to it.

When the group had assembled with Sherry, Susan, and Steve's mother in front, Preacher McMillan delivered the final prayer, "O God, by whose mercy the faithful departed find rest, bless this grave, and send your holy angel to watch over it. As we bury here the body of our brother, deliver his soul from every bond of sin, that he may rejoice in you with your saints forever." The casket was then lowered into the earth. Sherry leaned forward and tossed the white rose she had been clutching to her bosom onto the casket before slowly turning and being led away by Susan and Steve's mother.

I turned to leave and caught the eye of Donnie and Bill. "That was so sad," I said. "I feel so bad for Sherry. Losing a spouse after all these years." Donnie said, "Yes, it's such a shame. Sherry has always been the nicest person. We've lost too many of our classmates too soon." Bill added, "I tried to give Sherry my condolences, but I couldn't find the right moment. I'll have to see her at the wake. You know, it's strange, Donnie, Henry, John and I played a game of pickup basketball with Steve on the Friday morning of our Reunion last weekend, and Steve was still in great shape. I am having trouble processing how he could have died of a heart attack when he appeared to be in such good shape. Is it just me or does anyone else feel the same way?" Donnie responded, "He sure didn't look like he had any heart trouble to me." "Well, I guess we'll never know. It's something none of us plan for. We need to treasure the times we've spent together. Let's get together after the wake," I said as Gillian and I turned towards the parking lot.

After Gillian and I had expressed our deepest condolences to Sherry and her family at the wake, I said my goodbyes to my old track teammates and added that we needed to continue our planning for a post-reunion trip.

INTRODUCTION

CHAPTER 2

FAMILY

On the long drive back to Nashville, I had a lot of time to think about the unsettling events that had transpired over the last week. It had all started off happily with my great anticipation of seeing my old classmates again. I was in the kitchen with Gillian, my tall, attractive, silver-haired sixty-seven year old wife. Gillian called out "Connor" for the second time as I sat staring out our kitchen window unaware that she had already called my name once. Suddenly, I snapped out of my trance, turned towards Gillian and answered, "Yes?" Gillian, who had been cooking breakfast over the stove, replied, "I asked you if you would like pancakes with your eggs and bacon this morning." "Oh yes, thank-you Gillian," I said. Gillian returned to her cooking as I thought how lucky I had been to have married Gillian 43 years ago.

Those intervening years had been a wild ride with never a dull moment, and I had loved every minute of them. Gillian and I had been blessed to have raised three kind-hearted children, who had in turn provided us with three precious grandsons. We had also been blessed to have worked together in a rewarding dental profession for forty years before retiring in 2019 in our rehabbed home in East Nashville. Our actions now were not tied to anyone else's needs or schedules, and we were enjoying our "golden years" by reading, relaxing in our side-by-side easy chairs while watching the newest TV series, walking our dog, exercising in our water aerobics class, gardening, or traveling to Europe, Canada, and across the United States.

I was in a reflective mood. A lot had changed in the 50 years since I had graduated from my "middle class" High School, in Knoxville, Tennessee. Many of the changes occurred gradually and sometimes I didn't recognize how significant they were at the time. I was born on December 24, 1956, so I fall in the so called "Baby Boomer Generation," which was a result of the explosion of births right after the end of World War II. My upcoming reunion had given me a backward-looking perspective where I could more easily recognize the groundbreaking milestone events that have occurred in the United States during the lifetime of the Baby Boomer generation. There have been more than a few mind-boggling events. Besides the technological inventions that have made our life easier, the political and societal norms have come full circle from a conservative society in the 1950's to a progressively more liberal society from 1960 to 2016, and finally back to the current political climate that is trying desperately to take our society back to its more conservative past.

Knoxville is a Southern Appalachian college town that had a population of around 175,000 people in 1970 when I lived in the new West Knoxville suburb called Cumberland Estates. Knoxville sits in a valley between the Cumberland Mountains, 60 miles to the west and the Smoky Mountains 40 miles to the east. The French Broad River originating just west of the Eastern Continental Divide near Rodman, North Carolina, joins with the Holston River originating in upper East Tennessee near Kingsport, to form the Tennessee River at Knoxville. The Tennessee River flows past the University of Tennessee Neyland Stadium, past the wealthy homes along Cherokee Boulevard, continuing a southwestern trek to Chattanooga, where it turns westward passing through Northern Alabama before turning North to cross Tennessee and end its 886 mile journey by dumping into the Ohio River near Paducah, Kentucky. During the Civil War, Knoxville was home to a strong Union element. Following the war, many business leaders from the North established major iron and textile industries in Knoxville. Tennessee marble, extracted from quarries on the city's periphery, was used in the construction of numerous monumental buildings across the country, including Grand Central Terminal in New York and the U.S. Capitol. In the years after World War II, the University of Tennessee expanded ten-fold from 3,000 students in 1945 to 30,000 students in 1975, when I started college as a freshman.

I was the middle child of five siblings to parents who had settled in Knoxville after my dad had ended his career as an Air Force fighter pilot. I had two older sisters, Barbara and Paige, a younger brother, Ken, and a younger sister, Janet.

Barbara, my oldest sister, came of age during the late 1960's hippie generation that wore flowered dresses, attended the Woodstock Music Festival, experimented with marijuana and protested the Vietnam war. She was very headstrong and resented anyone telling her what to do, a trait that she got from her father. In fact, their headstrong temperaments butted heads when she was a senior in high school and she elected to go spend her final high school year with her maternal grandparents in Ocala, Florida. Predictably, after only one semester, she discovered that the grass was not greener at the home of her very strict Church of Christ following grandparents, and she returned to Knoxville for her last semester of high school. Barbara obtained her college degree at the University of Tennessee in Knoxville where she met and married Jeb, a music and journalism major. Barbara and Jeb had three daughters which they raised in Atlanta while Jeb was working for CNN. Barbara attended an Arts college in Atlanta and devoted her time to painting and creating artwork, including the making of jewelry after she and Jeb retired to Tallahassee, Florida. I never felt a close bond to Barbara. The five and a half year age difference was just too great, and Barbara had left the home by the time I was 12 years old.

Paige, my other older sister, was closest in age to me, and I always felt that we had similar intellectual pursuits and goals. Paige was very smart and easy to talk to. I also felt that the stars or the "powers to be" had aligned Paige and me in some way. Both our birthdays were celebrated as the day before Christ was born. Mine on December 24th is celebrated by most Christians and Paige's on January 6th is celebrated by orthodox Christians. Although Paige was born just shy of two years before me, she was only one grade ahead of me because her birthday fell after the first of the year and my birthday fell before the end of the year. In fact, we were even in the same French class when I was in the eighth grade, and she was in the ninth grade. Paige and I both ended up carrying on the family's tradition of practicing dentistry. After high school Paige obtained a dental hygiene degree at East Tennessee State University in Johnson City and worked for several years before applying to dental school. She was accepted to dental school and started her freshman year as I was starting my final year. Paige was elected President of her dental class, graduated third in her class, and got accepted to Periodontal School at the Medical

College of Virginia in Richmond, where she met and married Dr. Roger Bason, another dental student at MCV. Paige and Roger opened separate dental practices in Norfolk where they raised two sons. Tragically, Paige died at the age of 64 after falling and hitting her head on concrete, only two years after Roger died from early onset Alzheimer's disease.

Paige was 5'7" tall and had long straight blonde hair. Her slim figure and pretty smile got her elected as a cheerleader in Junior High School. But her interests diverged from cheerleading when she reached high school, where her intellect and her collegial, non-confrontational manner gained her many loyal friends, a trait she kept throughout her life. Paige was extremely perceptive, which led Tommy, one of her dental school classmates to say, "Paige could go in a room and read the mood better than anyone I have ever seen."

Despite my close feelings about Paige, she and I held widely different attitudes about certain societal norms. I am a "black and white" person, who tries to avoid gray areas. Perhaps due to her intelligence or boredom, Paige was prone to test society's rules. She made excellent grades, but she skated the line on what was acceptable behavior. As a teenager, she would sneak out of her window onto the roof and smoke cigarettes or drink beer, and she later moved on to experimentation with marijuana. She was clandestine about her questionable activities and maintained her "good girl" image. Like Carl Sagan and many other high achievers, Paige's use of pot never affected her academic or professional success.

Just as I couldn't understand why Paige wanted to smoke pot or occasionally "walk on the wild side," Paige had some trouble accepting my rather strait-laced attitudes. I just couldn't understand how someone would want to hurt their own body by smoking, drinking, or doing drugs. Nor did I have the inclination to question every law. I was happy with my life, and I didn't understand why some people were bullies or wanted to hurt others. I remember getting my first BB gun and trying relentlessly to shoot birds. When I finally hit one and it fell over dead, I felt so bad that I have never shot another animal.

It always bothered me that Paige called me "Jesus," insinuating that I was the "perfect child that never did anything wrong." I think it started as a play on my birthday, but it later proliferated into an indictment of my attitudes, beliefs, actions, and accomplishments. And maybe there was a little uncharitable intent there too. Maybe Paige was a little jealous or even frustrated that I was a fair-haired, smart boy with all the advantages that those adjectives endowed to boys of the Baby Boomer generation. I didn't smoke. I didn't drink. I played football and was popular in school. I was the Vice-President of my Senior High School class, and I got accepted into dental school. But I knew that I wasn't perfect and that placing me on that pedestal was unfair.

I'm not sure how much my older two sisters were affected by the societal norms at the time about what place women had in society, and how that affected their later career choices. They were primarily influenced by my mother, who was plenty smart, but who had had her first of five children at the age of 18, and who was frequently thereafter reminded by my father that she had no college degree. As was customary at the time for men of my father's generation, my father ceded all child-raising responsibilities to my mother. Until the age of 39, my father was flying almost constantly in the Air Force, having the time of his life, and showing up as a figure in his children's lives only during his brief overnight stays in between cross-country and international flights. Barbara was 14 and Paige was 11 years old before my dad left the Air Force and appeared at our home on a full-time basis.

For most of the time growing up, the children in my family would have had no one looking after their everyday needs if it wasn't for my mother Rita. She was a caring and hardworking woman who always put the needs of her children in front of her own. After all her children had entered school, she worked as a secretary, and later as office manager, for a local trucking firm for twenty years, using her income to ensure that her children had access to many of the nicer things in life. She made sure all her children got braces, her boys participated in football leagues, and her girls had the opportunities to participate in extracurricular activities.

My dad's cockiness and competitiveness made him the excellent fighter pilot that he was. Indeed, his desire to be the best pilot resulted in him being voted as the "Best Air Force Cadet Pilot" in his 1951G USAAF Aviation Cadet Class. However, the same independent characteristics that made him a good fighter pilot often conflicted with his ability to accept the occasional unfair criticisms of higher ranked, but less gifted officers, who were responsible for issuing his Officer Efficiency Reports (OER's). So, he was a prime candidate for RIF's that accompanied the military budgeting shifts from conventional manned airplanes to strategic nuclear weapons in the early 1960's. Even then, the Air Force gave my father the opportunity to stay in the Air Force in a "non-pilot" or "desk job" position to complete the 20 year requirement for a retirement pension. My father was so gung-ho about being a fighter pilot and all the cockiness that it involved, that he thought the suggestion of a "non-pilot" job was "ridiculous." Had my father been a long-term planner, he and his family would have been better served if he had "sucked it up" and stayed in the Air Force for four more years and obtained his retirement pension. But my father, who I suspect was probably on some kind of spectrum, had to live every minute of his existence to the fullest. He just couldn't conceive of having to waste four years of his life doing something that he didn't want to do.

CHAPTER 3

MOVE TO GRUNDY

As a result, my dad found himself at age 39 abruptly disassociated with his lifelong love affair with flying. He was over the age at which Commercial Airlines would hire pilots. He had no real job prospects and a family of five children to feed and clothe. My dad was under a lot of stress during the next three years trying to find a good job. When Barbara was between the ages of 14 and 17, and Paige was between the ages of 11 and 14, my dad went through a series of different jobs while accepting some financial assistance from his parents and his Aunt Lottie in Knoxville. He tried selling funeral plots, insurance, and used cars until his brother, who was a member of the Virginia House of Delegates, got him a job as Director of a new government assistance program in Grundy, Virginia that had been created by President Johnson's Great Society legislation.

My dad rented our house in Knoxville to a nice family and uprooted our entire family to the little town of Grundy in Southwest Virginia. We moved into the old home place of my grandparents. My grandmother was ill and lived in a residential home. My Grandfather moved into the apartment below his dental office. The move was quite a change for the children in our family. The raw beauty of Buchanan County was somewhat marred by the black coal dust that covered everything in sight, having fallen off the never-ending stream of coal trucks flying over the curvy roads.

The economy of the Appalachian area of Southwestern Virginia was almost exclusively centered on coal mining. Fluctuation of the markets, union strikes, mining accidents, and environmental damage by strip-mining all were associated with the industry. In addition, those families who didn't work in the mines frequently lived a squalid and poor life in the "hollers."

I attended the fourth through the seventh grades while we lived in Grundy. My classmates included one who had been crippled by Polio and one who had no electricity in his home. Many classmates still had outhouses for their bathrooms. Nonetheless, the people of Grundy were incredibly good-hearted people, and I thoroughly enjoyed roaming the mountains behind and in front of our house with my brother and my newfound friends. My father had time to participate in our lives and take my brother and me to our little league football team practice every day.

My dad's Director job in Grundy was political, so when my uncle left the House of Delegates and returned to his dental practice, the opposition party quickly replaced my dad with someone from their political party. My dad started selling insurance again and our only family car became a VW Beetle. After a while, my dad was offered a District Manager position in Roanoke, but my mother put her foot down and said that she wanted the family to return to our house in Knoxville, so that her children could have access to the University of Tennessee for their future college education.

CHAPTER 4

BACK TO KNOXVILLE

Four years after we had left Knoxville, we returned to our house in Cumberland Estates. My dad returned to car sales and quickly became the number one salesman for the next thirty years at the largest Ford dealership in Knoxville. I was 13 years old when my family returned to Knoxville. From that point onward, my family's financial situation began an upward climb towards a comfortable middle class home life situation. My siblings and I were beneficiaries of all the advantages that a middle-class lifestyle entails for the remainder of our time at home.

Ken, my younger and only brother, is a kind soul who was not as academically gifted as Paige and me. He was the only sibling who stayed in Knoxville after high school, and he has remained in touch with many of his high school friends. He followed our dad into the car business and became a finance manager at a local dealership. He likes to play golf with his friends in his spare time. He is a widower, having married twice, but sadly both of his wives died young.

My younger sister, Janet, developed a life-long love affair with horses at a young age. She couldn't decide on a major in college but finally got her degree in IT after attending Middle Tennessee State University in Murfreesboro for six years. She got a job in Atlanta, where she met and married Josh, a computer guru who had made a large amount of money in an IPO for a company for which he had developed medical office software. Josh bought a nice home with gorgeous horse stables in Winston, Georgia about 20 miles west of Atlanta for Janet, where they raised two boys and one girl. Janet spends all her time now raising Gypsy horses, under the protection of the LLC she created for her horse farm. Janet has a mercurial temperament and is known to "fly off the handle" over the most innocuous things. She is currently mad at, and not speaking to, any of her siblings.

CHAPTER 5

DAD AND MOM

My extroverted father, Harry, was always the center of attention in the family. He was a generous and hard-working man who was always active or excited about what he was doing, whether it was flying airplanes, developing the perfect golf swing, or selling a car. He was a friendly man genuinely interested in the lives of his customers, and he developed a very loyal following.

At the age of 47, during his spare time, my father started writing a memoir of his youthful experiences in Eastern Kentucky and Southwestern Virginia, and his subsequent flying experiences. He completed a rough draft of his book over the course of three or four years, but sadly, he never got an edited version published. After my retirement in 2019, I was fortunate to be able to edit his draft and publish his book entitled “From Kingdom Come to the Fringes of Outer Space.”

My dad monopolized all conversations by trying to share his excitement and his knowledge on how to sell cars, as if his impartation of car selling tactics would help all of his listeners better perform any of their endeavors or reach any of their goals. He involved his children in his favorite activities, automatically assuming that they would enjoy the activities as much as he did. But he was always teaching during his children's participation in those activities, whether it was showing them a bicycle trick, showing them how to throw a football, or showing them how to land the Cessna airplane that he rented from the Knoxville Flyers Club and in which he frequently flew his children. He enthusiastically enrolled several of his children in flying lessons at the flying club. Indeed, I soloed in a Cessna 150 at the age of 16 and later obtained my pilot's license at the age of 19.

I always wondered where my dad got his eternal optimism, especially since he had grown up during the depression in a very poor Appalachian area of Eastern Kentucky and Southwest Virginia. Moreover, my dad, at the age of 18, had to face the specter of being killed when he volunteered for the Air Force during World War II, and was sent to England as a waist gunner on a B-24 in the 8th Air Force. Notwithstanding, Harry always told his children that they could do or be anything they wanted. Any questioning of that premise would be met with his standard reply, "Can't never could do anything."

I can only surmise that my dad's confidence in success and his avoidance of anything negative must have been instilled in him early in his life by his parents and his Appalachian relatives. Harry's father was a dentist, whose father and grandfather had also been dentists. Harry's great-grandfather, Spencer, had been the first dentist in the family and had learned the art of dentistry by apprenticeship from his father-in-law. Spencer had returned to Lebanon, Virginia after his service in the Civil War as a cavalry man for the Confederate Army. Spencer's son, Arthur, learned dentistry from his father, and practiced dentistry in Inez, Kentucky, a small town near the Eastern Kentucky and West Virginia border. By the time Arthur's son, Harold, came along, dental schools had been established, and he earned his dental degree from the University of Louisville.

Times were tough in the Great Depression in 1928 when my grandfather Harold started his dental career, and he followed one mining town after another, starting in Eastern Kentucky and finally settling in Grundy, Virginia, the county seat of Buchanan County in Southwest Virginia. My father Harry was born in a small Eastern Kentucky town called PoorFork, which was close to Cumberland, Kentucky and the Kingdom Come State Park. Harry moved with his family to several Eastern Kentucky towns over the next few years until his father established his final dental practice in Grundy, Virginia when Harry was eleven years old. Harry continued to live in Grundy until he finished high school.

Doctors and dentists were sparse in the Appalachian areas where most men had limited education and worked in the mines or lived on small homestead farms. Thus, the few doctors and dentists in the Appalachian area were highly respected by the local people. Although Harry's father did not become wealthy and had to barter his services many times during the depression, Harry always felt that the community looked favorably upon him due to the respect that they gave to his father.

Harry's mother, Liz Caudill, was also a strong individual whose father was a part-time Baptist preacher and the owner of the General Store in Blackey, Kentucky. Liz's brother Jim had been a star center on the Centre Football team in Danville, Kentucky that beat the undefeated Harvard Football team in 1921, considered one of the biggest upsets in college football history.

Harry certainly got a large portion of his confidence from his successful and strong willed parents. But, to endure the many hardships confronting them, it was also a trait among the proud Appalachian people to glorify all good qualities and ignore all bad qualities. Harry learned to avoid discussing unfortunate events and to honor family loyalty among all else from his Appalachian relatives, friends, and neighbors.

My mother, Rita, was born in Southwest Virginia in a small town called Deel, which was only six miles up the Levisa Fork of the Big Sandy River from Grundy. She was the oldest child and only girl of very strict Church of Christ parents, who were of Scotch-Irish descent. Their ancestors had lived in the Appalachian Mountains for several generations. Rita's parents never went to college. Her father worked at various positions surrounding the coal mines, most frequently as a carpenter. Her mother worked as a beautician. Rita had four brothers, all of whom went into the Navy as soon as they turned 18 years old. Rita was quiet, but pretty and smart. She was very sincere in all her actions — some would say even stoic. She was only 17 years old when she met the charismatic Harry, who was seven years her senior and had seen the world as an enlisted soldier in WWII.

After the war, Harry had gone to Centre College in Danville, Kentucky, on the GI Bill, and had come back to Grundy to teach school. He met Rita at his father's dental office, where she worked as a dental assistant. A whirlwind romance ensued, and Harry and Rita were married soon thereafter. Rita has remained a devout Christian all her life and, through her actions, taught her children to never tell a lie and to always do the right thing. She and Harry remained devoted to each other and had been married for 65 years at the time of Harry's death in 2017.

CHAPTER 6

CUMBERLAND ESTATES

I attended Northwest Junior High School in Cumberland Estates, in West Knoxville with my siblings and the kids in the neighborhood. Swimming in the neighborhood pool, bicycle riding, playing sandlot football games, and playing basketball games at the Recreation Center were fun and frequent activities for me and my friends. The friendships I made with my local Little League football team would follow me all the way through high school.

One of my Little League football teammates named Blake became my best friend. Blake was a dark-haired boy of a bigger build than me, so he played tackle on the team while I played defensive back. Blake was a smart, observant kid, who couldn't resist making funny sarcastic remarks and chuckling whenever possible. I found him amusing and yet caring at the same time. I will never forget the time Blake was the only teammate who reached down to help me up in our high school junior varsity football game after I had taken a helmet to the rib, which later turned out to be broken. Blake had been in many classes with me in high school, including our sophomore Literature class with my favorite teacher, Mrs. Schultz. I still remember what an impact the novella "Portrait of Jennie" had on me.

Blake had attended the wedding of me and Gillian at St. Mary's Church in Memphis and had maintained contact with us over the years. He became a mechanical engineer, never married, and devoted considerable time to exercising, including swimming, running in marathons, and participating in triathlons. He was currently retired and living near Clemson, South Carolina, where he had tweaked his childhood preoccupation with mowing yards for money into a hobby and fascination with nurseries, with a focus on Japanese Maples. He had made trips to the Northwest United States, Nova Scotia, and Japan with fellow Japanese Maple enthusiasts to acquire more knowledge.

I enjoyed my time growing up in my tight-knit neighborhood, but my most pleasant coming of age memories happened during my time at West High School. West High was a wonderful school with great teachers and a bright and talented student body. I was smart and popular, and I frequently joined my friends in all kinds of fun and exciting extracurricular things like spelunking, camping in the Smoky Mountains, jumping off the water-filled rock quarry, and devouring the steamed ham and cheese hoagie sandwiches at Sam and Andy's Deli while cruising along the Cumberland Avenue strip. But my most enjoyable times revolved around my participation in the track and football teams during my three years of high school. The bonds I made while sweating it out on the football practice field or running around the track and along Cherokee Boulevard with my teammates would last me a lifetime.

So it was with great anticipation that I prepared to attend my upcoming 50th High School Reunion in Knoxville. I couldn't wait to reconnect with my track coach Jack and my old teammates like

Blake, Donnie, Matt, Keith, Bill, Henry, Jim, Ted, and John. We could revisit all the moments of fun, laughter, exertion, triumph, and disappointment that had been etched into our minds at that young and impressionable age.

CHAPTER 7

GILLIAN

After high school and college at the University of Tennessee in Knoxville, I went to dental school in Memphis, where I met Gillian, one of my dental school classmates. Gillian was pretty, smart and funny. I had never met a girl as straightforward and honest as Gillian. She always told everyone exactly what she thought. She could be critical yet compassionate.

In October of 1973, during my Senior year in High School, Columbia Pictures released one of the great romantic films, "The Way We Were" starring Robert Redford and Barbra Streisand. Robert played Hubbell Gardiner, a carefree, popular college student who felt no need to push any particular agenda because things had always come too easily to him. Barbra played Katie Morosky, a fiery, outspoken college student who was always ready to fight for some issue in which she believed. In short, Katie wanted to "rock the boat," but Hubbell couldn't understand why every issue required a full-on attack. I've always felt that I was like Hubbell and Gillian was like Katie when we first met in dental school.

Gillian attributes the differences between herself and me to our very differing childhood experiences. According to Gillian, my childhood was very "all American" in most ways. I was a very overachieving youth, and my friends were also overachievers. I was lucky to go to a stellar high school. I was a good athlete, better than most and so were my friends. I was a class officer dating a cheerleader. It all seemed normal to me. I never questioned the situation or the fact that there were very few blacks going to my school. I worked very hard and felt that I deserved what I got.

Gillian had a very different childhood. Like me, she came from a family of five children, one boy and four girls. She was the baby of the family. She was raised Catholic, and I was raised in the Church of Christ. Her father was an air traffic controller. Both our fathers served in the Air Force during World War II. My father was younger and entered the war as a waist gunner on a B-24 bomber plane after Gillian's father entered the war as a P-47 fighter pilot. The war in Europe ended before my father experienced many of the horrors of World War II. Gillian's father flew 67 missions over the Po Valley of Italy, which had exposed him to darker experiences.

Gillian remembers her childhood living with her dad as a totally different childhood than I had living with my dad. She had attended parochial school through the sixth grade. Money became a problem when her brother started college. Her father, a southerner, believed in educating the son, so all four daughters were pulled out of parochial schools and sent to one of the worst public schools in Memphis. Gillian always says that she quit learning anything new at the end of the sixth grade. Her school after the sixth grade was a huge "waste of time."

Gillian's father believed that women should marry, and he refused to pay for college for the girls. Gillian worked her way through college with a hodgepodge of jobs and what little money her mother could provide. But college was a real breakout moment for Gillian. She realized that she loved learning, and she took college hours just to learn new subjects. She would have gone to college forever, but the school said she was way over her hours and needed to decide what her career was going to be. She realized that she wanted to always be able to provide for herself, and she never wanted to ask a man for money. Dentistry would provide that living.

Gillian and I both started Dental school as the youngest in our class. There were 166 students, twelve women and the rest men. Gillian and I sat next to each other in the first class. A middle-aged pudgy teacher came in, pointed at Gillian, and asked her name. He then stated to the class, "Would one of you please marry her and give her the MRS degree she so wants." That would set the tone of abuse particular to women in their class, but Gillian always pointed out that the emasculation of the men in their class was just as overpowering.

Gillian's strengths complement mine. She colors between the lines, whereas I am very "black and white." It didn't take long for Gillian and me to become best friends and to later fall in love.

Gillian and I got married right after graduation from dental school and spent the next thirty years raising our son and two daughters in Memphis. Along the way, Gillian and I obtained our law degrees by attending night law school at the University of Memphis Law School, and we served eight years as Dental Officers in the U.S. Army Reserves during Desert Storm.

While keeping our noses to the grind in our challenging dental practices, Gillian and I still managed to remain involved in our children's activities, which included horseback riding, travel ice hockey games, scouting activities, and summer camps. Our family enjoyed regular summer vacations to the white sandy beaches of Destin, Florida and several winter vacations to the snow-covered ski slopes of Big Sky Montana. After the kids had left home, Gillian and I retired in 2019 to East Nashville where we rehabbed a house with the help of our son.

CHAPTER 8

CHANGING TIMES

As the time for my reunion got closer, I began to reflect on how the times had changed over the past 50 years. There had been a tremendous number of technological and societal changes during that time. The technological changes were easy to discern, like the internet, cellphones, computers, artificial intelligence, new medical and drug discoveries, and finally cars. I thought of my first car, a used 1969 VW Beetle, which cost only $1,900.00 new, but had no seat belts, no automatic transmission, no automatic windows, and no air conditioning. My recently purchased Subaru cost $40,000, but had front and side airbags, cruise control, lane assist, automatic braking, and automatic shut off when stopped in order to save gas. More and more of the recent cars being sold were hybrid or electric cars.

However, it was the social and political changes that bothered me the most. As I pondered how society had progressed from 1950 to 2010 and where the focus was today, I was troubled. It seemed that America's progressive march for more freedom and understanding had come to a screeching halt in the last decade and had, in fact, taken a turn backwards toward lesser freedoms and lesser empathy. Rather than being on an ever-improving arc, it seemed that my society's progress was on a pendulum, and the pendulum had started to swing back the other way.

I was born only 11 years after World War II ended. My generation grew up with a keen appreciation of how much our parents had been affected by WWII. Sixteen million Americans, or just over 10% of Americans served during WWII, including my father and both parents of Gillian. Gillian's mother served as a Red Cross worker in England and France. My generation referred to our parents as "The Greatest Generation."

My country has made great strides in civil rights since the end of WWII. In April 1947, Jackie Robinson, who had also served in the military during WWII, was the first black person to be allowed to play in Major League Baseball. And in July 1948, President Harry Truman integrated the United States military. It seemed that further progressive measures were sure to follow.

However, having survived both the Great Depression as children and the dangers of WWII as young adults, the "greatest generation" soon focused on returning their lives to normalcy. They started their families and tried to enjoy some of the economic growth after the war that led to widespread home ownership, suburban development, and relatively good times during the 1950's. Their generation was too busy achieving the American dream to concern themselves with the disparities among women, minorities, and the poor. Indeed, they didn't question the separate water fountains for blacks, the return of women to their role as homemakers after the war, and the economic and educational deprivations of the poor.

My parents grew up in the Appalachian Mountains of Southwestern Virginia, where the miners' struggles and impoverishment were glaring.

Outhouses and illiteracy were rampant in the hollers of the Appalachian Mountains. Gillian's father grew up on a farm in the South in North Carolina, where segregation was the norm.

Fears of nuclear holocaust during the Cold War kept the American public concerned primarily with harmonious political discourse. The first vestige of real societal change was prompted by the Earl Warren Supreme Court's ruling in Brown versus Topeka Board of Education, in May 1954, that the "separate but equal" doctrine set forth in the 1896 case of Plessy v. Ferguson was unconstitutional. It seemed to me that this holding was a demonstration that the United States would continue the struggle it had begun in the Civil War towards making American society a more equal and fair one. Notwithstanding, it would take several years and many more struggles before the implementation of this ruling would be carried out, especially in the Deep South.

One year after the Brown decision, which was one year before I was born, Black people were still required to sit in the back of the bus. In December 1955, Rosa Parks' refusal to give up her seat in the front of the bus in favor of a white passenger inspired the Montgomery bus boycott. The NAACP filed a lawsuit, Browder v. Gayle, that ended with a decision in November 1956, one month before I was born, that segregation of the races on buses was unconstitutional under the Equal Protection Clause of the 14th Amendment.

The call for more progressive freedoms for all American citizens continued in the early 1960's by leaders such as Dr. Martin Luther King, Jr. and John Lewis. In February 1960, when I was just three years old, four black students at North Carolina A & T University started a sit-in at the whites-only lunch counter in the Woolworth's store in Greensboro, North Carolina. Similar sit-ins in Nashville attained desegregation of downtown department store lunch counters in May 1960.

In May 1961, when I was four years old, civil rights workers called "Freedom Riders" began riding interstate buses with black people in southern states where the federal desegregation rulings were being ignored. It was not until September of 1962, when I was five years old, that the University of Mississippi admitted its first black student, James Meredith, which resulted in riots that were only put down when President John F. Kennedy sent in 31,000 federal troops.

Civil rights were not the only concern of the United States in the late 1950's and early 1960's. America was dealing with the Cold War tensions with the Soviet Union. Nuclear war was a big concern and schoolchildren, including me, were being taught to hide under our desks in case of a nuclear attack. These tensions were exasperated on May 1, 1960, when CIA pilot Gary Powers was shot down over Russia in his U-2 spy plane. President Eisenhower would first deny that the U.S. had been spying over Russia, but he had to admit his lie when it turned out that Russia had captured Gary Powers. Incidentally, Gary Powers lived up the road from my father while growing up in Buchanan County, Virginia. Gary's father bartered for dental services with Harry's dad. Gary would later graduate from Grundy High School.

I was four years old when the Cold War tensions came to a head in October 1962 with the Cuban Missile Crisis. After six years of guerrilla warfare in Cuba, revolutionary Fidel Castro overturned the dictatorship of Fulgencio Batista, on January 1, 1959. Castro soon earned the ire of the United States by implementing many socialist measures and nationalizing American owned oil companies without compensation in June 1960. Before he left office, President

Eisenhower approved CIA officer Richard Bissell's covert plan to invade Cuba and overthrow Fidel Castro. Newly elected President John Kennedy was convinced by the CIA to go through with the covert plan. On April 17, 1961, the covert Bay of Pigs invasion of Cuba failed disastrously. As a result, Fidel Castro turned to the Soviet Union for future protection, and the Soviet Union began to place missile sites in Cuba.

The "Cuban Missile Crisis" occurred from October 16 to October 29, 1962 when President Kennedy was advised by the CIA that Soviet President Nikita Khrushchev was sending nuclear warheads to arm those Cuban missiles directed at the United States, President Kennedy set up a ship blockade around Cuba to stop the Soviet ships from delivering the nuclear warheads. All Americans held their breaths as the Soviet ships steamed toward Cuba. Only the frantic last minute negotiations whereby the U.S. secretly agreed to remove offensive weapons it had placed in Turkey prevented a nuclear war and caused the Soviet ships to turn around.

Six months after the Cuban Missile Crisis, America's focus was again directed towards civil rights. In May 1963, when I was six years old, leaders of the nonviolent Southern Christian Leadership Conference organized peaceful demonstrations in one of the most segregated cities in the U.S., Birmingham, Alabama, to try to stop discrimination in employment, public facilities, restaurants, schools, and stores. SCLC organizers ran low on adult volunteers and decided to use high school and elementary school students on the protest marches to City Hall. The American public watched the sickening spectacle on TV when Birmingham Mayor "Bull" Connor called for the use of high pressure water hoses and police attack dogs on the children.

One month later, June 11, 1963, Alabama Governor George Wallace stood in the doorway of the University of Alabama attempting to block the integration of the school and the admittance of two black students. He only moved away after President John Kennedy and his brother Robert Kennedy, as U.S. Attorney, federalized the Alabama National Guard, which commanded Governor Wallace to step aside.

On August 28, 1963, black leaders organized the March on Washington for Freedom and Jobs, during which Dr. Martin Luther King, Jr. made his famous "I have a dream" speech. Decrying America's tardiness to make good on the substance of Abraham Lincoln's Emancipation Proclamation of 1863, Dr. King said, "I still have a dream, a dream deeply rooted in the American dream — one day this nation will rise up and live up to its creed, 'We hold these truths to be self-evident: that all men are created equal.' I have a dream."

President John F. Kennedy was tragically assassinated on November 22, 1963, when I was six years old. After Vice-President Lyndon Johnson was sworn in as President, he realized that something had to be done to alleviate poverty and racial injustices, so he pushed through a series of Civil Rights bills deemed "The Great Society" from 1964 to 1968. Major new federal programs were launched to address civil rights, education, medical care, urban problems, rural problems, and transportation. The Civil Rights Act of 1964 prohibited racial segregation in schools, public spaces, and workplaces. The Economic Opportunity Act of 1964 created the Jobs Corps. The Food Stamp Act of 1964 provided low-income people with assistance in purchasing food. The Social Security Amendments of 1965 created Medicaid, which funded some medical costs for low-income individuals, and Medicare, a health insurance program for people aged 65 and over. The Elementary and Secondary Education Act of 1965 authorized federal expenditure on schools with low-income students. The Voting Rights Act of 1965 ensured that minorities could exercise their right to vote. The Motor Vehicle Air Control Act of 1965 limited motor vehicle emissions. The Housing and Urban Development Act of 1965 expanded the federal housing program. The Civil Rights Act of 1968 prohibited discrimination against housing.

It seemed that the American public was being dragged, either willingly or unwillingly, into a freer and more egalitarian society. However, even the measures of The Great Society could not move fast enough for the long discriminated against black population, and race riots erupted in several major U.S. cities, including the 1965 Watts riots in LA and the 1967 race riots in Detroit and Newark. The assassination of Dr. Martin Luther King, Jr. on April 4, 1968, when I was eleven years old, prompted another round of race riots in Chicago, Baltimore, and Washington, D.C. Gillian was living in Memphis when Dr. King was assassinated there, and she remembers vividly how martial law and a curfew were implemented.

External events continued to spur along the country's march towards a better and more empathetic society. The futility of the ill-advised Vietnam War, which required a Selective Service draft of American men between the ages of 18 and 25 from 1964 to 1973 and resulted in the death of over 50,000 American G.I. soldiers, led to many protests at college campuses across the country.

The My Lai Massacre of innocent Vietnamese citizens on March 16, 1968, the dreadful televised spectacle of young anti-war demonstrators being Billy-clubbed by the Chicago police during the August 1968 Democratic convention, and the tragic shooting of protesting students on the Kent State campus on May 4, 1970, ultimately turned the American public's support against continuing the Vietnam War. It seemed that our country was adopting a more open view of international relations when President Nixon normalized relations with China in 1972.

As I approached the age of 18, I became acutely aware of the draft requirements surrounding the Vietnam War, during which 2.2 million American men were drafted out of a pool of 27 million. The last draft call was on December 7, 1972, when I was just shy of 16 years of age. President Richard Nixon ended America's involvement in the Vietnam War by signing the Paris Peace Accords on January 27, 1973. The Watergate break-in scandal resulted in President Nixon being the first president to resign from office on August 8, 1974, when I was 17 years old. President Ford was sworn in as president and pardoned Richard Nixon on September 8, 1974.

When I turned 18 on December 24, 1974, I registered for the Selective Service. The last drawing for the lottery was done on March 12, 1975, and depending upon the lottery number called for my birthday, I could have been called to report for induction in 1976, had the draft persisted. President Ford eliminated the requirement to register for the Selective Service on March 29, 1975. The requirement for young men ages 18 to 25 to register for the Selective service was reinstated on July 2, 1980, by President Jimmy Carter.

Women also were demanding more freedoms around this time. In 1971, the feminist movement, spurred on by figures such as Gloria Steinem, Betty Friedman, Bella Azbug, and Shirley Chisholm, began to demand more rights for women. At that time women could not obtain a credit card or a house mortgage in their own name. The Ivy League colleges were just beginning to accept their first women students. It was not until the October 28, 1974, passage of the Equal Credit Opportunity Act of 1974, when Gillian had just turned 18 years old, that women could obtain credit cards in their own name.

When Gillian was 15 years old, women's opportunities in sports took a great leap with the passage of Title IX of the Education Amendments of 1972, which prohibited discrimination in schools that received funding from the federal government. Gillian was 16 years old on January 22, 1973, when the U.S. Supreme Court decided the case of Roe versus Wade, wherein women gained control of their reproductive rights and the right to have an abortion.

Despite these successes for women's rights, the Equal Rights Amendment (ERA) failed to be ratified by the necessary 38 states by the original deadline of March 22, 1979. Congress later extended the deadline to June 30, 1982, but no additional states ratified it within that time.

The LGBT community was one of the last groups of Americans to gain the freedom to live their lives as they desired. On June 26, 2015, when I was 58 years old, the U.S. Supreme Court decided the case of Obergefell v. Hodges, which held that same sex marriage was legal and a fundamental right under the due process and equal protection clauses of the 14th Amendment.

America's exploration of space during the 1960's also created many memorable moments. On April 12, 1961, when I was four years old, the Cold War space race heated up when Soviet astronaut Yuri Gagarin became the first person in space. Ten months later, on February 20, 1962, John Glenn became the first American in space. The space race culminated on July 21, 1969, when two astronauts from the American spaceship Apollo 11, Neil Armstrong and Buzz Aldrin, became the first men to walk on the moon. Armstrong's famous words were, "One small step for man, one giant leap for mankind."

In the entertainment category, I recall that, although they had never been a favorite of mine, the Beatles music group came on the scene between 1963 to 1966, when I was between the ages of six and nine. I felt more deeply about Elvis Presley's death on August 16, 1977, because Elvis was from Memphis, and I had sadly missed the opportunity of catching a glimpse of Elvis in Memphis by just two weeks. I started dental school in Memphis on September 1, 1977.

Other impactful memories of significant political events during my early years include the shocking assassination of Robert Kennedy in Los Angeles on June 5, 1968, while he was running for President. I was eleven years old at the time. Another political event of equally shocking import occurred many years later when I was 32 years old, when protests brought about the fall of the Berlin Wall on November 9, 1989. Many people attribute the fall of the Berlin Wall to President Ronald Reagan's strong foreign policy and his famous spoken words while in Berlin on June 12, 1987, "Mr. Gorbachev, tear down this wall." However, I have always believed that Ted Turner had more to do with it. Ted, who had gone to the same all boys' military boarding school of McCallie in Chattanooga as had my cousins, had expanded his Atlanta based advertising conglomerate using satellites in 1976, and had created a 24/7 multinational news broadcasting network called CNN. I believe that once the East German people began to see how life was better in the West through CNN's broadcasting, they began to push for more democratic reforms. Two years later, on December 26, 1991, when I was 35, the Union of Soviet Socialist Republics (USSR) broke apart.

CHAPTER 9

SPORTS

As for the sports category, I have many notable memories. I participated in many sporting activities in my youth and admired many sports heroes along the way. My father always admired boxer Muhammad Ali, who was from Louisville, Kentucky. I was seven years old when Cassius Clay won the Heavyweight Boxing title by knocking out Sonny Liston on February 25, 1964. Cassius converted to Islam, changed his name to Muhammad Ali, and lost his title three years later on April 28, 1967, when he refused to be inducted into the military during the Vietnam War on religious grounds.

Ali explained his decision to decline military service with these words: "Why should they ask me to put on a uniform and go 10,000 miles from home and drop bombs and bullets on Brown people in Vietnam while so-called Negro people in Louisville are treated like dogs and denied simple human rights? No, I'm not going 10,000 miles from home to help murder and burn another poor nation simply to continue the domination of white slave masters of the darker people the world over. This is the day when such evils must come to an end. I have been warned that to take such a stand would cost me millions of dollars. But I have said it once and I will say it again. The real enemy of my people is here. I will not disgrace my religion, my people or myself by becoming a tool to enslave those who are fighting for their own justice, freedom and equality. If I thought the war was going to bring freedom and equality to 22 million of my people they wouldn't have to draft me, I'd join tomorrow. I have nothing to lose by standing up for my beliefs. So I'll go to jail, so what? We've been in jail for 400 years."

With respect to my favorite sport, football, I have a lot of special memories. I played quarterback on my little league football team and was extremely excited to watch the very first Super Bowl, which was played on January 15, 1967, when I was ten years old. The NFL's Green Bay Packers with Bart Starr as quarterback and Vince Lombardi as coach defeated the AFL's Kansas City Chiefs. The Packers would win the second Super Bowl the following year against the AFL's Oakland Raiders.

I clearly remember the 3rd Super Bowl played on January 12, 1969, when I was twelve years old, because I was in the hospital after having contracted pneumonia from playing too often and too long in the snow that had fallen in Grundy that December. I was confined to my hospital bed and there was nothing to do but watch TV, which was tuned into the Super Bowl game on NBC, one of only three national networks. The NFL's Baltimore Colts with Johnny Unitas as quarterback were highly favored to beat the AFL's New York Jets led by brash young quarterback Joe Namath. Joe surprised everyone with his pre-game "guarantee" of a win. "Broadway Joe" delivered on his promise and was named MVP when his Jets won the game.

Residents of Knoxville have an almost obligatory duty to wear orange and support the athletic teams of the University of Tennessee Volunteers.

My mom was a big follower of the Coach Pat Summitt-led Tennessee Women's basketball team, which won eight national championships. I had always been a big fan of the University of Tennessee football team and had attended many games at the 100,000 + seat Neyland Stadium. In fact, my first fun job after the newspaper route I had delivered on bicycle in Grundy, was selling cokes in Neyland Stadium at the age 13. I got to make some money and watch my favorite team. Sure, my apron got awfully sticky from spilled cokes, but I got to watch my heroes of the 1969 UT defensive unit, including their three awesome linebackers, Jackie Walker, Jack "Hacksaw" Reynolds, and Steve Kiner. One of my claims to fame was that I got to play a quarter of a football game on the artificial turf at Neyland Stadium during a high school jamboree tournament when I was playing for West High School.

As I thought back to those early days, I began to see a pattern of change regarding the participation of black athletes in SEC sports. The 1969 UT football team had only two or three black players, including Jackie Walker, who had been recruited by Coach Doug Dickey out of Fulton High School in Knoxville. Lester McClain was the first black player to play for the University of Tennessee in 1967. Kentucky had been the first SEC team to allow a black player on their football team two years earlier in 1965. Alabama was the last SEC team to integrate their football team after a thrashing in 1970 by an integrated University of Southern California team.

In 1971, when I was 14 years old, the University of Tennessee football team started Condredge Holloway as the first black quarterback in the SEC. In 1998, black quarterback Tee Martin led the University of Tennessee football team to its sixth and most recent national championship. Today, over one-half of the starters on the University of Tennessee football team are black players.

When I was in high school, I used to go over to the University of Tennessee's Tom Black track field for training runs. The University of Tennessee Men's track team had very good runners and won the National Outdoor championship in 1974, my senior year at West High School.

As for Olympic athletes, I was 15 years old, when American swimmer Mark Spitz won seven gold medals in the 1972 Munich summer Olympics. Four years later, when I was 19 years old, I watched with amazement while the petite Romanian gymnast, Nadia Comaneci, scored a perfect 10 and won three gold medals in the 1976 Montreal summer Olympics. Nadia would win two more gold medals in the 1980 Moscow summer Olympics, which the United States boycotted to protest Russia's invasion of Afghanistan. In 1989, Nadia defected from then-Communist Romanian before its revolution in December of that year.

Greg Louganis was another American Olympic athlete who astonished me with his skills and athleticism. Greg was the first diver to sweep all diving events in consecutive Olympics in 1984 and 1988. In between those two Olympics, I had the privilege of seeing Greg dive from the high dive and springboard at the University of Tennessee aquatic center while Greg was competing at an event there. Greg's incredible spring and smooth, flawless form were a wonder to watch. Greg would later do much to abate the abhorrence for AIDS by the general public when he came out as gay in 1994 and announced that he had AIDS. I was 27 years old at that time.

As for basketball, I remember the famous players when I was around 12 years old, like Wilt Chamberlain, John Havlicek, and Pistol Pete Maravich. Wilt was 7'1" tall and was said to have been an incredible athlete in high school in both track and basketball. He still holds the record for being the only professional basketball player to score 100 points in a game. I also enjoyed watching Wilt play with the Harlem Globetrotters.

As for John Havlicek, he was of Czech and Croatian descent, and he won a collegiate National championship while playing with the Ohio State Buckeyes in 1960. He played his entire 16 year professional career with the Boston Celtics and was known for his hustle and legendary stamina. He was an NBA All Star 13 times.

Pete Maravich, with his floppy socks, was an unbelievable offensive shooter. He starred at LSU where his father was the basketball coach. Even without the 3-point shot, he holds the all-time leading NCAA Division I scoring title with 3,667 points scored and an average of 44.2 points per game, and that does not include a freshman year, since freshmen were not allowed to play on the varsity team at that time. He tragically died at the age of 40 from an undiagnosed congenital heart defect.

More recent basketball players that I remember include Kareem Abdul Jabbar, who at 7'2" in height, won three straight NCAA championships with UCLA from 1966-1969 when he played for Coach John Wooden and went by the name of Lou Alcindor. Another great player who faced Kareem Abdul Jabbar in his professional career included Indiana native, Larry Bird, who played for the Boston Celtics.

CHAPTER 10

REUNION PLANNING

After I finished reflecting on the significant events of the past 50 years, I noted that Gillian and I had better make the hotel reservation soon for my upcoming high school reunion in Knoxville. "How many days should I reserve the hotel, Connor," asked Gillian. "Let's start with a couple of days and see how it goes. I may want to stay and visit a little longer. We'll just play it by ear," I responded. Gillian understood and made the reservation at the Marriott Residence Inn. She had become used to our flexible schedule during our retirement.

Gillian and I loved to travel and had been doing a good bit of it in the past few years since our retirement. We had just recently returned from a fun thirty day excursion with our dog Rex in our old, rehabbed camper around the Great Lakes and the scenic Upper Peninsula of Michigan. We had rounded out that trip with visits to our older daughter, her husband, and two of our grandsons in Madison, Wisconsin, and then our younger daughter in Chicago. Earlier in the year we had visited Northern Ireland and Scotland before ending our international trip with a stop in Stockholm, where we spent some time with our son, his wife, and our third grandson.

Since I had been Vice-President of my Senior class, it fell upon me by default to take charge of organizing our 50th Reunion, along with Lynn, another classmate who had attended the 1973 class's reunion with her older sister and was familiar with the venue and arrangements. The President of my Senior class, Bob, who had spearheaded the 20 year reunion, was still working full-time as a radiologist, and had to defer the planning of the 50th reunion to Lynn and me.

Lynn and I started the search for the current addresses of classmates and had reserved the venue a year in advance. The search for female classmates was particularly challenging because so many maiden names had changed. Nevertheless, Lynn and I did a fairly good job of locating all but a few of our 240 class members. I was amazed at how many of my classmates had become engineers. A few had become doctors or lawyers, but the majority had remained in the Knoxville area.

One talented classmate, Ronnie, had followed his acting talents to New York City where he acted in several Broadway plays and won a Peabody Award. He lost a personal friend in the September 11th terrorist attack on New York City in 2001 and began to reevaluate his life. He stopped acting and became a monk with an Episcopalian religious community in Cambridge, Massachusetts for seven years. He returned to his hometown of Knoxville to care for his ailing parents. One day he stopped by Kroger's and bought a lottery ticket, little knowing that it would be a "winning ticket" that would change his life in a big way. He immediately took his significant winnings and set up a Foundation to support the love of his life, that being theater production in theaters all across the United States.

Sadly, about 15% of my classmates had died, including the tragic loss of a few to car wrecks or Leukemia shortly after graduation, and the recent loss to COVID of a cherished classmate who was looking forward to attending the reunion. Lynn and I established a reunion committee, e-mail communications, zoom meetings, and obtained volunteers for the various activities required — collecting money, signing catering contracts, decorations, and entertainment. Special efforts were also made to invite teachers and coaches who were still alive, and I was extremely happy that my track coach "Jack" had accepted our invitation to attend the reunion.

Coach Jack, who coached primarily track and cross-country, but also assisted in coaching the football team, was everybody's favorite coach. He was 6'2" tall with curly hair and long legs with unbelievably muscular calf muscles. He had been a track star at the University of Tennessee and still held a couple of school records. Although he was only 26 years old when he first coached me in high school, he seemed so much older and mature to the 16 to 18 year old kids he coached at that time. That ten year age difference from 16 to 26 was enormous, especially in the way of emotional maturity.

Coach Jack was completely dedicated to coaching, especially with the track teams. I will never forget how Coach Jack, who lived down the street from me, would drive me and a few other classmates to school at 5:30 am every morning, so that we could get an early morning practice run in before school started. Coach Jack was a born leader and mentor to so many classes at West High, and he continued to be involved in coaching and officiating track meets even up to the present time. He was the kind of coach that everyone should have! Everyone was extremely happy that they were going to connect with him again after so many years!

CHAPTER 11

50TH REUNION

Gillian and I rose early on Thursday morning to pack our burgundy colored Subaru Forester for the three hour drive to Knoxville. We wanted to get to Knoxville a day before the first reunion event — an informal get together at the Rocky Top Blues Cafe on Kingston Pike, which would be open to other classes besides mine. The formal Reunion event would be open only to my class and would be on Saturday night at The Foundry in downtown Knoxville. A tour of the greatly expanded West High School on Saturday morning would be guided by Colin, who had graduated two classes ahead of me and had later become a teacher, coach, and Principal at West High.

Gillian and I pulled out of the driveway at 8:00 am just after sunrise on Thursday, heading towards East Tennessee. I always enjoy the drive along I-40 towards Knoxville, especially in the fall when the leaves start to turn yellow and orange colors. The landscape is hilly and covered with so many trees. Tennessee is a very picturesque state. Once upon returning from a business trip to drought-stricken California, my daughter-in-law had remarked that, "Tennessee looks so green from the sky." My dad, who had flown jets over 42 countries including most in Europe, was always glad to return home to the beautiful mountains of East Tennessee, which he called his "little Switzerland."

The city of Knoxville lies in the valley between the Cumberland Mountains to the west and the Smoky Mountains to the east, the latter of which I could see on a clear day 40 miles away from my childhood home as I caught the bus for school in the mornings. At the time that I attended West High School, the population of Knoxville was about 175,000, and that number would fluctuate during school breaks when many of the 26,000 student body left the University of Tennessee Knoxville campus and returned to their hometowns. Several of the parents of the West High School student body worked as Professors at the University of Tennessee or as Doctoral scientists in one of the research facilities in Oak Ridge, home to the secret Manhattan Project during World War II where uranium was separated and converted into plutonium in the K-25, Y 12, and X-10 facilities.

Gillian and I drove through Cookeville, Tennessee, home of Tennessee Tech University about 100 miles east of Nashville. We lost an hour on the clock as we crossed over into the Eastern Time Zone around Rockwood and Harriman as we descended off the Cumberland Plateau. We continued driving by the Crab Orchard Limestone mines and TVA's Clinch River Nuclear Power Plant. We knew we were close when we passed the signs for Melton Hill Lake and entered the I-40/I-75 junction. We arrived at the Marriott Residence Inn in West Knoxville around noon EST. We checked into our room and then later went out for dinner at the Texas Roadhouse.

The next morning, I drove Gillian around my old childhood neighborhood, the West High School, and the University of Tennessee campus, admiring how much Knoxville had grown. New subdivisions were everywhere and much of the old businesses, including Sam and Andy's Deli on Cumberland Avenue, had been replaced by the University of Tennessee student housing. When I saw the expanded campus of West High School with its new track and bleachers, I could almost feel the sensation of sweat formerly streaming down my face when my teammates and I used to run 440's around the track and run up and down the bleachers. I was surprised to see that the old natural grass football field had been converted to an artificial surface, compliments of the Haslam Family Foundation and Haslam's former company, the Pilot Flying J, which had converted all thirteen Knox County School football fields into artificial turf. The Haslam family was well known in East Tennessee — one of the Haslam brothers, Jim, owned the Cleveland Browns Football team and the other brother, Bill, had been the Mayor of Knoxville and then later the 49th Governor of Tennessee from 2011 to 2019.

Around 2 pm, I took Gillian out to the relocated Sam and Andy's Deli on Kingston Pike near Cedar Bluff exit and ordered a couple of steamed hoagie sandwiches. I just couldn't pass up another opportunity to enjoy my teenage delight in those mouth-watering sandwiches. We returned to our hotel and changed into clothes for the Friday evening event at Rocky Top Blues Cafe.

Gillian and I pulled into the Rocky Top Blues Cafe around 7 pm. We were directed to the outside covered room where several of my classmates were sipping their drinks and noisily reconnecting with old friends. Donnie recognized me and shouted, "Hey Connor, how are you doing? Long time no see!" I responded, "Hey Donnie! Good to see you. You're looking good!" Donnie was still his tall, lanky self. I can still picture Donnie giving his determined effort in the two mile race and then cracking up the rest of his teammates later with "Ron and Don Wright" professional wrestler imitations or his imitation of Kareem Abdul Jabber during their pickup basketball games. I asked Donnie, "Are you still running?" Donnie responded, "No, my knees gave out. I have had both replaced." Donnie and I continued to catch up with what had happened in our lives over the last 50 years. Donnie's dad had flown in the Knoxville Civil Air Patrol with my dad. Donnie had recently retired after working many years as a Sheriff's Deputy and as an Air National Guard Reservist. He had flown all over the world with the Tennessee Air National Guard and had especially enjoyed his flights to Alaska. His two daughters had inherited his height and athletic prowess and had gone through college on volleyball scholarships. Donnie and his wife lived in Knoxville but had purchased a condo in Atlanta, where they could spend time with their grandchildren. I caught Donnie up on the happenings in my life, including my three children and three grandsons.

About that time, Ted, another track teammate, came over and said, "Connor! How are you doing man!" Ted, another tall lanky miler who used to approach the four minute mile mark in high school, had put on a little weight. I reminded Ted of his former running feats by asking him, "Hey Ted, what is your mile time now?" Ted laughed and said, "Not like the good ole days at West High." I caught up with the events of Ted's life, which included a lot of time now devoted to fishing, and then I continued to work my way around the room where a continuous hum of conversation was occasionally interrupted with a loud guffaw or exclamation.

I spotted Mitch and said, "Hey Mitch, thanks for putting this Friday event together. Where is Steve?" Mitch and Steve had hung around together in high school where they were golf teammates. Mitch, who was loud and always at the center of things, and Steve, who was a mischievous basketball star, were always up to something in high school.

Steve was the guy who had enticed me and Blake to accompany him to the rock quarry and jump off the cliff into the water 50 or 60 feet below. I will never forget that event. Steve wanted the three of us to hold hands while we jumped together. I wanted to jump by myself for the first time to see how it went, so I went ahead and jumped first. Not knowing that I should keep my legs stiff, I was extremely lucky that I had not knocked myself out when both of my knees recoiled up on either side of my head as soon as I hit the water. Steve was angry that I had not waited to jump together, so he started throwing rocks at me below. I had to dive under the water to keep from getting hit by the rocks. But Steve soon tired of his little game and then jumped off the cliff with Blake.

Steve had also cajoled me and a few other classmates to drive out in the country one night and look for the ghost that supposedly crossed the road in front of the car as we passed the designated rock. Steve's enthusiasm and encouragement was hard to resist. When I had given the reunion information to Greg, another classmate and good baseball player, Greg had recounted the hilarious story of Steve talking Greg into accompanying him on a graduation night celebratory fishing adventure. They had trouble getting onto the lake and ended up falling asleep in their car. There was never a dull moment when Steve was around!

Mitch and Steve had continued their association after high school by becoming partners in the purchase of a laundry mat. Mitch leaned in close to me and said, "Listen, don't tell anybody else this, but Steve and I had a falling out. I sold my share of the laundry mat to Steve, but he later failed to pay me what was due. I guess he is embarrassed or something, but he has kind of dropped off the map. I've tried to stay in touch, but he doesn't talk to me or any of the old gang anymore. I doubt he'll come to the reunion." I was a little disappointed because I had wanted to rehash some of the crazy exploits instigated by Steve.

I continued around the room and found Lydia, an honor student in high school who had become a nurse anesthetist. She was still working and loved her job. She had married a couple of times, and she introduced me to her current husband, Bill, who was a film producer originally from England. When I mentioned that I had just published my dad's memoir posthumously about his Air Force experiences in World War II while stationed in England, Bill asked me what type of plane my dad had flown in. I told him that my dad had been a waist gunner on a B-24 named "Wandering Wanda" while stationed at Old Buckenham Field in East Anglia. Bill quickly replied that his father had piloted a British Lancaster bomber during that war. "Small world," I thought to myself.

Gillian started a conversation with Lydia about their mutual careers in the healthcare field but soon disengaged from the conversation when Lydia went on her rant about "being tired of people trying to take away her guns." Tennessee is a 70% Republican voting state and "gun rights" are a priority for the majority of those voters, many of whom are avid hunters. Gillian and I, both of whom have served as Army Reserve Officers, are on the other end of the political spectrum and believe that the Second Amendment did not guarantee the right of citizens to own rapid-fire machine gun type weapons, which have been used in several recent mass shootings, including the one at an elite private school in Nashville last year. Unfortunately, the Republican controlled Tennessee legislature continues to block all attempts at stricter gun control measures.

I exchanged greetings with several more of my classmates. I had hoped to see some old friends from other classes at the Friday night event, but the turnout was somewhat disappointing. I had wanted to reconnect with my close football teammates from the class of 1975, like Luke, Sam, and Owen, but I guessed that they were waiting on their own 50th reunion the following year. I had heard that Luke was in Texas, Sam had become a college president in Kentucky, and Owen had become an Air Force jet pilot who eventually obtained the rank of General. I anticipated seeing more people at the main event the next night at The Foundry, where 110 alumni and guests were expected.

The Friday night event was still in progress when Gillian and I left the event to return to our hotel. It had been refreshing to see the old faces — most of which were readily recognizable, despite the other changes in outward appearance that the passage of 50 years tended to place on one's body. The gray hair, loss of hair, and/or weight gain sometimes shocked me, but the personalities were undeniably the same as in high school. I enjoyed reconnecting with my classmates and had a smile on my face as I retired for the night.

CHAPTER 12

WEST HIGH SCHOOL

The next morning Gillian and I had breakfast at the hotel and then headed for West High School on Sutherland Avenue. Gillian let me out so I could attend the school tour with my classmates while she drove to the recently modernized downtown area to visit the Saturday morning farmer's market, always a pleasurable activity for her.

As I was walking inside the front door, I ran into my old track teammate, Matt, with whom I had been corresponding prior to the reunion because Matt lived in Wisconsin and my older daughter had moved there last year with her family. It turned out that Matt's wife and my daughter had similar motives in moving to Wisconsin— to escape the oppressive Tennessee Republican agenda to take away women's rights in Tennessee.

Matt and his wife had no children and were avid enthusiasts of running, bicycling, hiking, and other outdoor activities. In fact, they had both recently bicycled across the entire United States. Matt had not changed much — his 5'7" frame was still thin, and his hair was still blond. He had been a distance runner in high school, and he had never stopped running. He told me that he had participated in numerous marathons and triathlons, climbed Mt. Kilimanjaro, and had an upcoming trip planned to climb Mt. Rainier in Washington state. After hearing about all of Matt's activities, I jokingly asked him, "Do you still have all your natural joints?" To which Matt chuckled and said, "Yes, but I have a piece of metal in the sole of my foot where I wore out a bone fragment with all my running." Many of my classmates had knee or hip replacements.

Matt and I entered the lobby of the high school where about 50 of our other classmates had assembled to hear the pre-tour guide instructions given by Colin and the current School Principal. I said hello to as many of my classmates as I could quickly recognize and then we were led through the greatly expanded and modernized academic classrooms. Only the old auditorium appeared to have kept its original form. As we were led outside to the track and field area, Matt said to me, "I got here early and ran eight miles on the track already this morning." I dropped my jaw in awe and said, "That's incredible! You must be in the best shape of any of our classmates."

Soon, other old track teammates came over and joined me and Matt and began to rekindle our long-ago camaraderie. Donnie was the first to come over. He greeted everyone and started with his impressions of Coach Jack, who wasn't in attendance, but who we would see later that evening at The Foundry. Next, came the dual high jumpers, Bill and Henry, both of whom amazingly cleared close to seven feet while competing in high school track meets.

Both Henry and Bill had maintained their slim builds. Bill had opened a private detective agency after retiring from the police force in Knoxville, Tennessee. He played a lot of golf in his spare time and had recently posted a Facebook photograph of him after he had shot a hole-in-one.

Henry had walked on to the University of Tennessee's track team for his freshman year along with Keith, another high school classmate who was a shot putter. Henry quit the team in his second year to focus on his academics and later obtained his PhD in School Psychology. He rose to the level of Superintendent of the Nashville District secondary schools several years before his retirement last year. He and his wife had no children but attended many professional and collegiate sporting activities and concerts around the Nashville area. He regularly posted his artistic photographs of various birds and animals that he had photographed in Nashville's Radnor Park. He also made regular trips to Knoxville to visit his now 99 year old Greek mother, who was healthy and as mentally sharp as she had ever been. Henry had a very dry sense of humor and used it to keep Coach Jack on his toes. Henry cracked me up when he said, "I went up and thanked Ronnie for saving me a lot of money on lottery tickets, because once I heard that someone from our class had won the lottery, I knew that the chances of any other classmate winning the lottery were next to zero."

Keith was still his jolly, stocky self, although his hair was now gray. He was still working as a medical device salesman in Knoxville, but he planned to retire at the end of next year. He was very vocal in expressing his happiness about reconnecting with everyone at the reunion.

John, who had run the low hurdles with me in high school, had obtained a Minister's degree and had established a Methodist Church in the small town of Dayton, Tennessee. The rural town in southeast Tennessee was famous for having been the site of the 1925 "Scopes Monkey trial" involving Darwin's theory of Evolution and pitting attorneys Clarence Darrow against William Jennings Bryan. John, who had also maintained his slim build, was very nice and diplomatic, perfect attributes for a Minister.

Jim was a tall shot putter who had also played on the football team with me and his younger brother Luke, who was in the class behind us. Jim had become a successful businessman in Atlanta, and he gave me an update on what Luke had been doing in Texas over the years. I had been closer to Luke because we were both defensive backs, while Jim had been an offensive lineman.

Finally, Blake joined his teammates and was shortly recalling some of our gridiron memories. "Hey Connor, remember how our Senior football team failed to win a game? Can you believe that the West football team has won the state championship the last two years?" I replied, "That is some kind of improvement!"

The high school tour was fun and lasted about two hours. It had brought nine or ten of my old teammates back together again. The old bonds were rebuilding with every recollected story and the subsequent laughter among the teammates. It seemed that the fifty year gap had vanished, and we were back in high school again when everything was so new and impressionable. The old team couldn't wait to continue the "esprit de corps" at the formal dinner that evening.

CHAPTER 13

AN UNEXPECTED DEATH

Gillian picked me up after I summoned her on the phone, and we returned to the hotel to rest before the big Saturday evening dinner. A few hours later we had changed into our evening clothes and were driving downtown towards The Foundry, a meeting place near the golden Sunsphere that had been built during the 1982 World's Fair in Knoxville. We were one of the first couples to arrive because I wanted to hook up my computer to the venue's projection screen so that my continuous PowerPoint presentation could be seen by the attendees. Gillian and I walked in and were greeted by Lynn who was quickly darting between the memorabilia table, the caterers, the table settings, and other volunteers to make sure all the arrangements were in order. Classmates LuAnn, Toni, and Patty had outdone themselves with the table and flower decorations and the obituary tree, which had small hanging photos of all our classmates who had died.

I quickly connected my computer to The Foundry's audio-visual system, and the many photos I had uploaded from my School annual began to appear on the large screen at the front of the room in five second intervals. Current photos of classmates were also shown beside the original school annual photos for an interesting comparison. I thought it odd how many of the classmates posed with their heads tilted the exact same way in both the new and the old photos even though there was a 50 year gap between the time that the photos were taken.

Soon, all attendees had arrived, and more heartfelt greetings were heard all across the room. The PowerPoint presentation and the Reunion booklets were a hit. Everyone enjoyed reading the short biography about each class member in the Reunion booklet. So many classmates had finished their careers and were spending time with grandchildren, traveling, or working on their various hobbies. I had fun going around the room talking to classmates I had not seen in a very long time and posing for small group photos taken by the hired professional photographer.

Matt and I cornered Coach Jack for several minutes, expressing our fond memories and appreciation for all that Coach had instilled in us. I said, "You know Coach, I always thought you were older than you really were at the time. How old were you when you coached us?" Coach responded, "I was 26 years old and had only been at West High for four years when I first coached you guys." I inquired almost to myself, "How were you that much more mature than we were?" Matt began describing his life-long running activities to Coach and I said, "See what dedication you instilled in us Coach?" Matt said, "That is right Coach. I owe all my achievements to your mentorship at old West High." About that time, Bill and Henry called Coach over to visit them for a while. Donnie, Bill, Blake, and John joined them in their old war stories.

To my surprise, Steve showed up at the reunion after all. I walked over to Steve who was regaling Bill, Henry, and Donnie with one of his stories. "Hey Steve, it's good to see you! I had heard that you weren't coming," I said. "What? Did you think I would pass up an opportunity to revel in the glory of my high school basketball playing days?" responded Steve with a laugh. "Seriously, what are you doing now," I asked. "After I sold my laundry business in Colorado, I moved back to Knoxville. I'm into a lot of things. I piddle in the stock market and cryptocurrency, and Sherry and I just bought a nice home out in Farragut. What about you, I heard that you're in Nashville," Steve said.

I quickly gave Steve a summary of my life after high school and then our conversation turned to our teenage escapades. "Remember when we used to go to the Recreation Center and play basketball and shoot pool?" I asked. "Yes, and sometimes I'd make out with Samantha behind the building," Steve responded with a chuckle. "Yea, we sure were young," I said. "Samantha was the first girl that I ever kissed. She had the cutest dimples." We continued recounting memories until it was time to find our seats.

After about 45 minutes of greetings, everyone found their tables and sat down for dinner and a few words from Bob, the class President. Gillian and I sat at a table with Matt and his wife, Donnie and his wife, Blake, and Coach Jack. Bob welcomed all the guests and thanked the Reunion Committee for all their work in making the event possible. He thanked those who had donated to the Reunion fund and then asked all who had served in the Armed Services to stand up to accept a round of applause. Donnie, Gillian, and I stood up from our table. Bob then asked all to have a moment of silence for our deceased classmates. Finally, Bob gave a small speech about how neat it was that our high school bonds had remained so strong some 50 years later.

We ate our nice catered dinner and continued catching up with those at our table. Blake, who was always health conscious and watched his weight, skipped the ice cream dessert then chuckled when he saw me accept Gillian's dessert after I had already devoured my own dessert. After we finished our dinner, someone called up all the track teammates who were present to have their photograph taken with Coach Jack. It was a classic photo op that saw Coach Jack sitting in the middle with ten beaming teammates standing beside him, five on each side.

Before we knew it, it was nearing the end of our reserved time. I turned to Blake and said, "This has been a lot of fun, and I don't want it to end. You know what? We should plan a group trip like the '73 class did last year. Eight teammates from their class took a week long rafting trip down the Colorado River to celebrate their 50 years of friendship. We could ask the ten teammates who were in our photo with Coach Jack if they would be interested in planning a rafting trip or hiking trip somewhere exciting for a week or two." Blake quickly chimed in, "That's a great idea!" "What do you think Donnie?" I asked. "I'm game," replied Donnie. "Count me in too," said Matt. "Let's run it by Bill, Henry, Ted, and John," I said.

Blake and I went over to Henry's table and presented our proposition. All the teammates at the table were enthusiastic about doing something like that. "OK, let's start planning it," I said. "We'll have to think about where we want to go and what we want to do. Let's go back to our hometowns and think on it for about a week and then open the floor for suggestions." Everyone agreed and we were just getting ready to leave when we heard a big commotion a couple of tables over.

Sherry let out a scream and yelled, "Someone call 911." We turned our heads and saw that Steve had collapsed on the floor and Bob was administering CPR. Everyone at Steve's table was standing around in shock or asking what happened.

The ambulance arrived within minutes and Steve was carried out on a stretcher. Sherry accompanied the ambulance to Ft. Sanders Hospital, which was just a couple of miles away. Blake and I asked Bob, "What happened? Is he going to be all right?" Bob looked at us grimly and said, "I don't know. It appears that he went into cardiac arrest." Everyone slowly made their way to the exits, still wondering how their perfect reunion had so suddenly ended on a tragic note.

CHAPTER 14

POST-REUNION TRIP PLANNING

On the return drive to Nashville the next day, Gillian and I learned that Steve had died. It really shook me to think that I had just been talking to Steve about old times. I experienced a brief jolt of my own mortality when I thought that Steve was my age. I said to Gillian, "We'll have to return for his funeral. I feel so bad for Sherry."

A few days after Gillian and I returned to Nashville, I asked her, "Now that Steve has died, do you think I should cancel the idea of going on a future reunion trip with my track teammates?" Gillian responded, "No, if anything, Steve's death should make you more determined to reconnect with your high school friends while you can. You're not getting any younger."

I let Gillian's words sink in for a few days as we received word that Steve's funeral would be this coming Saturday at Cedar Bluff Presbyterian Church in Knoxville. We made a new hotel reservation and started back to Knoxville on Friday morning. The sadness of our journey dampened our ability to enjoy the scenery along the drive.

As Gillian and I were passing the Melton Hill Lake sign, I said, "You know, I think I am going to ask the guys to continue our planning for a post-reunion trip after the funeral. Most of us are retired and can get away for a couple of weeks. We shouldn't waste an opportunity to do this trip while we're still in good health." Gillian said, "I think you're right to go ahead with your planning. What kind of trip do you think you would take?" I said, "I've been thinking that we could go on a rafting trip like the '73 class did, or we can hike a section of the Appalachian trail. We could visit someplace like Costa Rica where we could snorkel in the water and ride the zip lines in the mountains." Gillian said, "Those all sound like good ideas. I'm sure you all will come up with the perfect trip."

After Gillian and I had attended Steve's funeral and returned to our home in Nashville, I was in my kitchen having breakfast when I got a call from Henry. "Hey Connor, let's meet for lunch," said Henry. "I've got a great idea for our trip. Can you meet me at J. Alexander's tomorrow at 12:00?" "Sure, I've got some ideas as well," I said.

The next day, I entered J. Alexander's at 11:50 am and immediately saw Henry already seated. I walked over, shook Henry's hand, and said, "Nice recommendation for lunch. I've always liked J. Alexander's." Henry was all smiles as usual and said, "it's one of my favorites too, albeit a big step up from our old high school hangout at the Krystal's on Kingston Pike, right?" I chuckled and sat down.

The waiter came over and took our order. When the waiter left, I said, "What did you come up with for our excursion plans?" Henry said, "You're not going to believe this, but my mother owns a cottage in a small little town on the southern coast of Crete called Treis Ekklisies — it means Three Churches. The cottage has been in the family for years and passed down to her when her parents died. She must keep it up and usually hires someone to stay there for a time once a year to make sure everything is in order. It's a cute little town with white concrete cottages stacked up along the coastline and a short distance up the side of the steep, rocky Asterousia Mountains that jut all the way to the water's edge in most places except for little harbors like Treis Ekklisies. The town dates to the Minoan civilization before Roman times and is incredibly scenic with expansive views of the deep blue Mediterranean Sea.

It's very peaceful and, although there are about 50 cottages in the village, there are only 34 full time residents. Most of the cottages have been refurbished and many are rented out as AirBNB's. There are four seaside cantinas that are open during the busy season when several small boats come into the harbor for the day. The weather is always beautiful and it even stays around 55 to 60 degrees Fahrenheit during the winter months. There are many hiking trails nearby that include archaeological finds from early Minoan times. Little white Greek Orthodox churches, goats, sheep, and olive trees dot the surrounding countryside.

We could get our teammates together, go over to Crete for two or three weeks in October, stay at my mother's cottage, and have a great time experiencing the adventures of that exotic place, as well as, the Mediterranean diet and the happy, slow paced living exhibited by the Cretans. October is great weather for hiking their amazing trails, and the summer vacationers will have already left. We'll have the place almost to ourselves. And the kicker is that my mom's parents set up a trust fund for the care and upkeep of the cottage, and this trust fund could pay for all expenses, including the round trip airfares for all of our teammates. What do you think?"

I was flabbergasted and responded, "Wow, you're really thinking big! It sounds amazing, but I was thinking of something a little closer, like hiking the Appalachian Trail. Do you think our teammates would go for something that exotic? I mean relaxing on the beach and hiking the trails surrounding a little Cretan village sounds wonderful, but is it too far-fetched?" "I don't think so," responded Henry. "I mean how many more opportunities are we going to have to get all of our old teammates together in one place and in good enough health to take those adventurous hikes? So, why not go for the gusto? All we can do is ask our teammates if it's something they would do."

I thought about what Henry had proposed all the way home. It was a great opportunity, but really — Greece? Would our teammates go for it, I wondered. I drove in my driveway, got out, and walked over to Gillian, who was in her sun hat working in her raised bed gardens. Gillian loved experimenting and watching all kinds of flowers and plants grow. I had never seen her leave a Lowe's store without browsing through the garden section for marked down flowers. Just as I reached her, Gillian carefully planted her last cabbage and turned towards me. I gave her a kiss on the cheek and said, "You're not going to believe what Henry proposed today for our teammate trip!" "What did he say?" Gillian asked. I proceeded to tell her all about the Crete opportunity. As I finished, I asked her, "What do you think? Do you think it is too much of a stretch to ask my teammates to go to Crete for our trip?" Gillian said, "No, it sounds exciting, and it would be a once in a lifetime opportunity. Go for it!" I was already feeling a lot better about the idea, and I said, "You're right. You're always right. I need to get the ball rolling and get the rest of the guys on board." We went inside and I started making phone calls to my teammates.

"Hello," said Blake as he answered his phone. "Blake, this is Connor, how are you doing?" I said. "I've got some good news that I want to run by you." "Sure, what's up?" asked Blake. I blurted out the proposal that Henry had proffered over lunch. "What do you think Blake? Would you be game to take an all expense paid, once in a lifetime trip to Crete with nine of our old track teammates, where we could hike, go camping, relax on the beach, or cruise along the seacoast in a sailboat?" Blake didn't hesitate, "Absolutely, I wouldn't miss it for anything! The hiking and water activities sound perfect to me. I've never been to Crete, but I'd sure like to go." I said, "I figured you would want to go, so I called you first. Now, I'll just have to get the rest of the guys on board. I'll make some more calls and get back to you. Talk to you later."

Henry, who was retired and had made the proposal, was definitely up for the trip. Bill, his best friend, readily agreed to go on the Crete excursion. Donnie and Matt, retired and always up for adventure, said that they would go. John, who had a very flexible schedule as a Minister, also agreed to go. Only three of the ten teammates had to decline. Keith couldn't go because of his work. Ted had to stay because he was caring for his wife, who was in ill health. And Jim couldn't go because his youngest daughter was getting married on October 8.

I called Henry and told him that seven teammates would be going on the trip. Henry finalized all arrangements with his mother to have the cottage available. It would easily accommodate all seven track teammates. Roundtrip airline tickets were purchased and a three row van was rented from a small car rental agency at the Heraklion Airport.

CHAPTER 15

SHERRY'S CALL FOR HELP

Two weeks before my teammates and I were scheduled to fly to Crete, I got a call from Sherry, Steve's widow. "Connor," she said, "I desperately need your help!" "Sure Sherry, I'd be happy to help you anyway I can. What is wrong?" I responded. "The medical autopsy found that Steve was poisoned. The life insurance company is refusing to pay, and the police think that I killed Steve for his life insurance policy. You know me and you know that I loved Steve. I don't care about any life insurance policy, and I would never have killed him. You've got to help me prove my innocence. I know you're a lawyer and you're the only one that I can trust to help with this terrible situation," said Sherry.

I was momentarily speechless, but I regained my composure and said, "OK Sherry, I'll do anything I can. I'm leaving on October 1st on a three week trip with several of my old track buddies, one of whom is Bill Boyer. Bill is currently a private investigator, and he can help us get to the bottom of this. Keep sending me all the details and I'll talk to Bill. We'll see what we can find out. In the meantime, do you have a lawyer? I'm not a criminal lawyer, but I can connect you with a good criminal law firm in Knoxville. Don't say anything to the police without your lawyer present." "Thank-you so much Connor. I'm sorry to bring all this on you right before your trip, but I didn't know what else to do," said a somewhat relieved Sherry.

As I said my goodbye to Sherry, my mind was spinning. "Steve poisoned?" I thought. "Who would have wanted to kill Steve?" I needed a copy of that autopsy report ASAP. I thought I knew Sherry well enough to believe her when she said that she wouldn't have killed Steve, but stranger things have happened. I would have to be very careful in any investigation into Steve's death. Hopefully, Bill would be able to assist me in getting to the bottom of Steve's murder.

I called Bill and explained what Sherry had asked me to do. Bill was as surprised as I was that Steve's death was being investigated as a murder by poison. I asked him if he could use his private investigator experience to help establish that Sherry didn't kill her husband. Bill couldn't believe that Sherry could be culpable, and he quickly agreed to help. "We need to see who had a motive to kill Steve," Bill said. "We need to start interviewing family, friends, and classmates as soon as possible. We can do some work by phone and internet while we're on our trip, but we need to hit the ground running as soon as we get back. We should enlist Donnie in our investigation. He still has contacts at the Knox County Sheriff's Department who might provide us with updates." "OK," I said, "I'll talk to Donnie."

CRETE

CHAPTER 16

FLIGHT TO EUROPE

I couldn't believe how quickly the last week of September arrived. The airline tickets to Crete had a departure date of October 1st, and I had made sure that all my teammates had their passports up to date and had obtained the new ETAS permit that would be required for travel in the EU by non-residents.

Blake called me two days before we were to depart and inquired, "Should I bring my Cinch tent?" I said, "No, we can buy a tent over there. They have hiking clubs there, so I'm sure they'll have everything we need. We need to keep our luggage to a minimum." Blake said, "OK, I just want to make sure we're properly outfitted for some awesome hiking adventures. Are Donnie and Henry all packed up?" "Yes, they both called me yesterday and said they were excited and ready to go. Everyone else has confirmed that they'll be in Knoxville the day after tomorrow for the 3 pm United Airlines flight to Naples. It'll be a long flight with a connection through Frankfurt, Germany."

Gillian had opted to stay at home in Nashville and take care of the house and dog. She could tend to her garden and keep up her water aerobics classes. I was grateful that Gillian had no reservations about me reconnecting with my old teammates in such a novel way. Gillian had seen the pictures of the incredible scenery in Crete and said, "You all are going to have stories to tell for the rest of your lives about this adventure!" I told Gillian, "I'll FaceTime you when we need to talk. We'll have Wi-Fi at the cottage, but I may be out of touch when we go on hikes. I'm going to purchase an international health insurance policy just in case I might need it. I'll miss your excellent cooking skills, but I'll make do and maybe even discover a new favorite Mediterranean food. Remember, I discovered goulash in Norway." Gillian was a little skeptical and said with a laugh, "I hope you don't lose too much weight over there."

Gillian and I left Nashville around 9:30 am on October 1st for me to catch the 4:30 pm United Airlines flight to Naples. Gillian would drive the car back to Nashville by herself. I was wearing my hiking boots and had managed to squeeze all my clothing and accessories into one mid-size luggage carrier. Given the expected mild October temperatures in southern Crete between 55 and 65 degrees Fahrenheit, I didn't need to pack any heavy winter clothes. I figured that the most I might need was a light rain jacket and a fleece jacket for hiking the surrounding rocky mountain ranges rising from the coast.

Gillian and I pulled into Knoxville around 1:30 pm and picked up some Sam and Andy's steamed hoagie sandwiches before continuing to McGhee-Tyson Airport, some 13 miles south on Alcoa Highway. Gillian parked in short term parking and accompanied me and my luggage into the terminal building. "Hey Connor, over here," shouted Donnie who was standing around Bill, Henry, Matt, and John. "We've already checked our bags and we're just waiting for you." Gillian and I walked over and exchanged greetings.

"I'll be right back," I said. "I'm going to go check my bag." I walked over to the United Airlines counter, checked my bag, and then returned to join the group, who had found some seats near the terminal entrance. Henry was busy showing photographs of his mother's cottage and the surrounding scenery in Treis Ekklisies. "See those steep rocky mountains? There are numerous hiking trails going up and all over those mountains that we can climb. The views are outstanding. Just look at that view of the Mediterranean Sea. We can plan fishing and boating activities as well. You all are going to love it!" "Are there places where I can make my early morning runs?" asked Matt. Several teammates groaned and Bill said, "I'm more interested in how close the cantinas are to the beach."

"It's time for us to go through security," I said. I turned to Gillian and gave her a long bear hug and said, "Thanks Gillian! Be careful on the way back to Nashville. I love you and I'm going to miss you. I'll let you know when we get there." Gillian kissed me and said, "Have fun and be careful. I love you too." She then turned and headed out the front doors of the terminal. I started walking towards the security checkpoint with my teammates.

All the teammates made it through security smoothly except for Donnie and Matt, who had to be individually scanned because of the metal in their knee and foot, respectively. We headed down the terminal corridors in a group towards our United Airlines gate. I was talking to Matt, "It's too bad we're not flying with Emirates Airlines — they really provide top rated service. I flew on Emirates once to Europe and the seats were very roomy, the food was excellent, and the attractive stewardesses looked very professional with their red pillbox hats with connecting white scarves." Matt said, "Yes, I agree. Of all the airlines I took while I worked for a company in Germany for a couple of years, I liked Emirates Airlines the best." Donnie said, "Any luxury will be welcome compared to my time flying in a C-17 Globemaster III with the Air National Guard." Blake added, "The Boeing 787 I flew on to Japan with my Japanese Maple tree nursery friends was very nice."

Bill and Henry were discussing the prospects of their upcoming trip. "It's too bad Coach Jack is not coming. We could really have some fun teasing him again," said Henry. "Yes, so true," said Bill. "But it's great to get all our teammates together again. It feels like old times when we were traveling to away track meets. Do you speak any Greek, Henry?" "Only a perfunctory amount like Hello, Goodbye, and Thank-you, but Google translate really comes in handy. You should download the Greek language to your phone while you're in the states," responded Henry. Bill said, "Good idea. I bet you can't wait to take some stimulating photographs while in Crete." "Yes, I read that Treis Ekklisies is home to a large colony of vultures, including the bearded vulture and the griffon vulture. The Ambas Gorge cliffs near Treis Ekklisies are the only habitat for bearded vultures in the area," said Henry excitedly. "I can get some great shots!"

Henry and John paired off and began discussing their expectations for their Cretan adventure. Henry said, "I'm looking forward to taking in some of the archaeological sites, like Knossos Palace, relaxing on a sunny beach, and soaking in some sun. I'm ready for an exotic vacation."

John said, "As a lifelong student of religious history, I'm looking forward to learning more about the Greek Orthodox religion. I'd like to attend some of the services in those little one room church chapels all over the area. I am fascinated by the historical transitions from the Venetian Roman Catholic religion to the Muslim religion, and then finally to the Greek Orthodox religion in Crete. From 1205 to 1669, the Venetians controlled Crete and built Roman Catholic Churches. After the Venetians lost the Cretan War (1645-1669) to the Ottoman Empire, the Ottomans converted the Roman Catholic Churches to Muslim mosques."

John continued with the historical facts, "From the 1500's to the 1900's the Muslim Ottoman Empire fought several wars with Christian Russia for control of the areas surrounding the Black Sea (Crimea, Ukraine, Armenia, and Azerbaijan), the Balkan countries along the Adriatic Coast (Albania, Serbia, Montenegro, and Croatia), Greece, and Crete. While the Ottoman Empire was successful in several early wars with Russia, it eventually became weaker and lost later wars and territory to Russia. However, the breadth of Russia's control never included Istanbul. The disastrous attempt by Russia and Great Britain to wrest control of Istanbul from the Ottoman Empire in WWI during the Battle of Gallipoli was the brainchild of Winston Churchill, and it hampered his military ambitions for the years between the World Wars."

John stopped to take a drink from his water bottle, then continued, "In March 1821, Greece won its independence from the Ottoman Empire, but Crete remained under Ottoman control. With the help of the Great Powers (Britain, France, Italy, and Russia), the Greek Orthodox population of Crete successfully revolted against the Ottoman Empire and gained Crete's sovereignty in 1898. The Muslim mosques in Crete were then replaced by Greek Orthodox churches. Today, 98% of the Cretan population identifies with the Greek Orthodox Christian faith. A peculiar tenet of the Greek Orthodox religion is that they do not worship three dimensional icons, because they feel these statues are too lifelike and will detract from devotion to the spiritual faith. I suspect it also had to do with wanting to differentiate early Christianity from the plethora of sculptures that were present during the pinnacle of the pagan pre-Roman Greek era. As a Methodist Minister, I have a keen interest in studying the differences between the Greek Orthodox religion and Protestantism."

Blake and Matt began discussing their various competitive running experiences after high school. Matt, who continued to have superlative times for his age group, said, "I ran the Boston Marathon twice and the New York Marathon three times. I've competed in countless 10k's across the country, but recently I've begun to focus on bicycling with my wife. It's easier on the knees."

Unlike Matt, Blake had not been a runner in high school. He had been a shot putter but later developed an obsession with running and exercising after high school. Being single, he devoted almost all his free time to training. He ran 3k's, 6k's, mini-marathons, and marathons. Always striving to achieve more, he added swimming and bicycling to his training regimen and entered several triathlons. "I've been to Lake Tahoe a couple of times. I did an Ironman distance triathlon there in 1985. They had relay teams and Greg LeMond was there and I met him. One of my friends did the Western States 100 miler and I drove vehicle support for him. He dropped out around 50 miles. I love that area," Blake told Matt.

The United Airlines representative began announcing boarding instructions at 4:00 pm. Donnie shouted, "Let's go team, saddle up!" One by one all the teammates boarded the plane when our boarding group was called. We found our assigned seats, which were arranged together in a group, and settled in for the first leg of the flight to Washington, D.C. We would board an international flight in D.C. to Frankfurt, Germany. We had a four hour layover in Frankfurt before boarding the final leg of the United flight to Naples, Italy. We had picked Naples as our final United Airlines destination because we wanted it to be our departure point back to the United States after spending our last few days in Italy exploring Rome, the Amalfi Coast, and Pompeii.

To get to Crete from Naples, we would fly RyanAir to Athens, where we would catch a Blue Star Ferry to Heraklion, Crete. We would reverse the ferry ride and RyanAir flight to get back to Naples from Crete on our return trip home.

The flight to D.C. only took a couple of hours. Donnie exclaimed, "Man, that landing was rough!" Matt and I agreed as we started for our next gate. Fortunately, we had plenty of time to get to the United Airlines gate for our Frankfurt flight. When our boarding time arrived, we entered the much larger Boeing 777 that had 10 seats in 3 sections across two aisles. "Now this is more like it," said Bill. Our seats had TV screens and a nice selection of movies for us to choose from on our nine hour flight to Frankfurt.

I settled into my seat and scrolled through the movie selections. Thinking I might learn something about Greek culture, I chose to watch "Zorba the Greek," an Academy Award winning movie based on Nikos Kazantzakis' novel, and starring actor Anthony Quinn as Zorba. Zorba was a vibrant, passionate, older Greek man who tried to teach his younger, reserved, intellectual boss to enjoy the simple pleasures of life despite the many misfortunes they encountered trying to make a go of the boss's startup lignite mine on the island of Crete. Although sometimes crude and impulsive, Zorba was known for his dancing, storytelling, and zest for life.

I enjoyed the philosophical dialogues in "Zorba the Greek." For instance, when Zorba was younger, he came upon a grandfatherly man planting an almond tree. Given the grandfather's age and the fact that he would probably not live to see it grow to its mature development, Zorba asks him why he's planting it. And the grandfather, bent as he was, replies, "My son, I carry on as if I should never die." Zorba replies, "I carry on as if I was going to die any minute." Zorba turns to his boss and asks him, "Who is correct?

I thoroughly enjoyed the movie, and my favorite part was when Anthony Quinn performed Zorba's dance, the sirtaki. After I had watched the movie, I could better understand the famous quote from the movie: "Life is trouble. Only death is not. To be alive is to undo your belt and [look] for trouble."

I watched another movie and then fell asleep. I was awakened by an airline stewardess, who asked me to raise my seat back and buckle my seatbelt as we would be landing in Frankfurt in about ten minutes. I looked around and my teammates were also getting ready for the landing. The plane's touchdown this time was smooth as silk. My teammates and I took our time getting off the plane because we had four hours before we boarded our plane for Naples. It was 10:30 am and we had arrived in the European Union. Donnie said, "Hey, I'm hungry. Anybody else want to join me in finding something to eat?" Several of the guys followed Donnie to the food court area in the very nice and modern Frankfurt terminal.

All teammates reassembled at our United Airlines gate around 1:30 pm. Although we were tired, we were determined to see our flight through to its final destination. That old team camaraderie bolstered our spirits just like it did when we were halfway through a competitive track meet back in high school and we knew we had to "suck it up" to complete the meet. We boarded the plane for what turned out to be a much shorter two hour flight to Naples. We arrived in Naples around 4:30 pm and retrieved our luggage, all of which had fortunately arrived. We took a shuttle to a hotel near the airport for a much needed restful night. Our RyanAir flight to Athens was leaving at 10:00 am the next morning.

I had purchased T-Mobile's international package before I left Nashville, so I called Gillian to tell her that I had arrived in the EU. Gillian was seven hours behind me, so it was 10:00 am in the morning in Nashville. "Hi Gillian! We made it to Naples with all our luggage." "I'm glad you made it. What time is it there?" asked Gillian. "It's 5 pm and we're at the hotel. We're tired and I'm going to sleep early. We'll fly out tomorrow on RyanAir to Athens," I said. "Well, get some rest and have a safe flight tomorrow. I love you," said Gillian. "Love you too," I said as I ended the call.

The guys and I arose early the next morning feeling much refreshed from our jet lag. After a nice breakfast together, we caught the shuttle to the airport. When I saw the long lines at the security checkpoint, I nudged Blake, "I'm glad we arrived early, aren't you." "Yes, and I'm glad I only have one piece of luggage," responded Blake.

We all made it through the security check and to our gate in time to board when our group was called. The flight took just under two hours, and we arrived at the Athens airport around noon. The extremely long walk to the baggage area was made more pleasant by the moving escalators and the numerous exhibits along the wall depicting interesting things to see in Athens - like the Acropolis, Temple of Olympian Zeus, the Parthenon, Dionysus statue, etc. There were columns every 25 feet or so along the moving walkway with an embedded video of people from every country - Poland, France, Belgium, Turkey, U.S., etc. saying a short blip of what they liked about visiting Athens. We finally reached the baggage area and received all our luggage a short time later.

My teammates and I were in no hurry and sat down at a cafe for a Cappuccino or cup of hot chocolate. We discussed how we were going to get to Piraeus Port to catch the Ferry to Crete. We had nine hours before the Ferry left at 9 pm. Since we had plenty of time, we decided to take the Metro. It turned out to be a good thing because we met some nice people and got to witness the kind and gentle spirit of the Greek people. Our Metro train ticket would not open the sliding window entrance gate, but a tall, young Greek man who spoke English with a heavy accent took great pains to explain that he had the same problem and had asked the attendant, who told him he just needed to follow someone else through the gate. So, my teammates and I took his advice and followed other people through the gate. We then got on the train where almost all the seats were taken. Blake, Donnie, Henry, and I found a seat, but Matt, John, and Bill had to stand. I started a friendly conversation with a young man probably 20 or 22 years old from Orleans, France. He had a short ponytail and an easy smile. He was well traveled and had many friends living in different countries. He was currently living in Geneva, Switzerland, but was going to Athens to visit a friend who had opened a restaurant there. He engaged us in an interesting and long conversation about world affairs and life in the United States. He had been to Nashville and had a friend who went to Belmont University. He had also visited Montreal and Quebec.

After the young Frenchman got off at his stop, my group and I were trying to figure out what stop to get off and a local man tried to help us. He told us that we needed to get off at the next stop and switch to the blue line. My teammates and I got off at the next stop with him and he went over to the other side of the track. He then realized that he had made a mistake, and rather than just let me and my teammates get onto the wrong train, he started yelling and gesturing at us from across the tracks for us to stay there and take the next train. He was determined to get us on the correct train.

CHAPTER 17

FERRY RIDE TO CRETE

We managed to catch the next train, which took us quickly to the port. There was a bus sitting there ready to drive us around the port to get to our Ferry. We followed a friendly couple who helped us with directions on the train onto the bus. Bill looked out the bus window and said, "Hey, there is the Blue Star Ferry sitting right across from the bus. These people must be riding on another Ferry." So, my teammates and I got off the bus and went over to the Blue Star Ferry. An employee told us, "This Blue Star Ferry is not your Ferry. This one leaves at 5:00 pm. Your 9:00 pm Ferry will be docked over there on the other side of the pier." My teammates and I decided to walk around the semi-circular pier to where our Ferry would be docked.

When we had walked about a half mile with our luggage, a taxi van stopped and offered us a lift. The taxi driver said, "I can take you in two trips." I asked him, "How much to take us the rest of the way to our Ferry?" The taxi driver said, "Ten Euro dollars is the minimum charge." My teammates were tired, and we thought that ten Euros was a fair price, so four of us loaded our luggage and hopped in the van. The taxi driver didn't know what Ferry line we were using until we showed him our digital tickets. He then discovered that our boat was only about 100 yards away. But to get to the boat, he had to drive around the circling road a ways. And, most importantly, he explained that our ship was not named "Blue Star," but was named "Anek." We would have wasted a lot of effort otherwise discovering that fact. He also told us that we could not board until 6 pm, but that we could wait in the cafe across the street until our boarding time. So, his services were well worth the $10 Euros, despite the short drive!

My three teammates and I exited the taxi and thanked the driver with the Greek thank-you "Efcharisto." I shouted back to the other three teammates, "Hey guys, it's just over here. Come on." They soon joined my group of teammates, and we started for the cafe to wait for our boarding times along with other passengers doing the same thing. The café staff were very friendly. The Greek people seemed non-stressed and readily willing to help you or let you go in front of them.

At the 6 pm boarding time, I saw some people lining their luggage up outside the ship by a trailer. I asked a very friendly family beside us how the process worked. The gregarious mother explained in detail the process as her friendly daughter also chimed in. Then the father made sure that my teammates and I got our luggage loaded by lifting them one by one to the handlers in the trailer. He did this before he attempted to lift his own luggage, even though he and his family had arrived at the trailer before me and my teammates. I felt humbled by their kindness, so I helped them lift their luggage, one of which was a portable keyboard - so one of them must have been musically talented. It was dark and raining slightly, but this kind family had no problems stopping their loading to help me and my friends. We would see this kind of hospitality repeatedly by the Greek people.

My teammates and I then boarded the Ferry and found our way to our assigned "airplane seats," which reclined and had good legroom. I sat across from a nice 25ish young girl from Crete, who began a friendly conversation with me about the differences in the Cretan culture and the American culture.

I noticed that many of the Greek passengers on the Ferry did not appear affluent. They wore clean, but inexpensive clothes, the predominant color being black. Many passengers slept on the floor or stairways of the Ferry on their rolled out blankets. Nevertheless, the Greek people were a proud people who did not seem unhappy or uptight. They were very friendly and quick to help. I would later see a much more affluent population in the nice Heraklion downtown district with its many shops and cafes. Indeed, some parts of Crete were frequently visited by celebrities and millionaires who wanted to enjoy the pristine and uncrowded beaches.

I periodically slept during the eight hour Ferry ride over to Crete. At one point around 2 am, I walked out on the deck under the several lifeboats hanging alongside the deck to stare out at the dark sea. The large Ferry, which was a cruise ship size, appeared to be traveling around 20 mph and causing whitecaps along its side.

CHAPTER 18

HERAKLION

Heraklion, which is on the mid-northern coast of Crete, is Crete's capital and has a population of 180,000. Crete is similar in size to the U.S. state of Delaware, but its entire population is only 625,000 people. One half of the entire population of Crete live in two cities, Heraklion and Chania, another popular port city on the northwestern coast of Crete with a population of 112,000. Thus, the remainder of Crete is sparsely populated and mainly agricultural or tourism based. Olive grove trees are ubiquitous in Crete and sheep and goats are scattered throughout the high mountains, a few of which are even snow-capped half of the year. Orange and lemon trees can be seen in the front yards of many cottages in the small villages.

The warm hospitality of the Greek people is well known, especially in small villages like Treis Ekklisies, which is on the southern coast of Crete a little over an hour's drive south from Heraklion through the wonderfully picturesque mountains and Messara Valley of central Crete. Any hiking and camping supplies can be obtained in Heraklion, while all foodstuffs needed while in Treis Ekklisies can be obtained in the small villages of Charakas and Pyrgos, just eight miles north of

Treis Ekklisies. The drive from Charakas and Pyrgos to Treis Ekklisies requires a meandering descent of the rocky mountainside facing the Libyan Sea, which is considered part of the Mediterranean Sea. The road going down the mountain includes twenty hairpin curves back and forth, which provide a glorious view out over the deep blue water as far as one can see.

We arrived at Heraklion, Crete around 6 am. It was dark, cold, and raining when my teammates and I retrieved our luggage and caught taxis to the Heraklion Airport, where we had reserved a van from an airport car rental company. We picked up our 10 seater rental van, which was a manual transmission like most cars on Crete. I became the designated driver because I was familiar with stick-shifts. We drove down the many narrow one-way streets to our hotel in Heraklion, the Astoria Capsis Hotel, where we would spend our first night in Crete. We were going to spend a few days enjoying the sites and Cretan cuisine of Heraklion before we headed to Treis Ekklisies.

Parking spots in downtown Heraklion were limited. Consequently, most cars were small, and motorcycles were abundant in the downtown area. Young and old motorcycle riders alike, many without helmets, would whiz by on either side of the cars. My teammates and I found an inexpensive AirBNB near the center of town for the remainder of our stay in Heraklion. We parked about a block away on the seaside drive. As we walked back to our AirBNB, we took in the refreshing view of the mountains in the distance and the magnificent waves that rolled in one after another in an apparently restless sea. The promenades of the downtown district lined with nice shops on either side reminded me of those I had seen in Lisbon.

My teammates and I spent the next couple of days in Heraklion walking among the busy promenades, perusing the many shops, sampling the Greek coffee, herbal teas, and cuisine in the sidewalk cafes. We also visited the farmer's market, which consisted of a half-mile long row of stands loaded with fresh vegetables, olives, figs, nuts, fish, and handmade cheeses. The gray haired and mustachioed Greek men who tended their booths would smile at my teammates and me, wink, and wave us over to the booths as they explained in the Greek language the redeeming qualities of their delicacies.

My teammates and I also toured several interesting sites while in Heraklion. We toured the statue and tomb of Nikos Kazantzakis' (famous Greek author of "Zorba the Greek"), and the Greek Orthodox Cathedral of St. Minus, where we admired its ornate murals, woodwork, and two dimensional icons. The Agios Minas Cathedral serves as the seat for the Archbishop of Crete.

On our second day in Heraklion, my teammates and I took a bus tour to the famous Knossos Palace, a Bronze Age archaeological site and major center of the Minoan civilization. During our viewing of the Palace, John blurted out, "I can't get enough of this kind of archaeological stuff!"

As John admired the bull-leaping wall fresco, he said, "I've always been fascinated with the Greek myth of Theseus and the Minotaur, which has its roots in the Minoan civilization. Theseus, a young prince of Athens, sets out for Greece to slay the Minotaur, a half-man and half-bull monster, who in accordance with a peace pact between King Aegeus of Athens and King Minos of Crete, has been periodically eating several human sacrificial Athenians. Theseus goes into the labyrinth, slays the Minotaur, and escapes the labyrinth using the ball of thread provided to him by King Minos' daughter, Princess Ariadne. Theseus falls in love with Ariadne, who returns to Athens with him," finished John.

CHAPTER 19

TREIS EKKLISIES

On Wednesday morning, my teammates and I loaded up our van for the 40 mile drive south across the island to the cottage of Henry's mother in Treis Ekklisies on the southern coast of Crete. The van started gradually gaining elevation as we left Heraklion, and we could see the sprawling little white concrete houses by the Mediterranean Sea disappearing behind us. We admired the scenic beauty of the huge mountains in the distance as we passed through the heavy agricultural production areas.

Henry said, "Agriculture and tourism are the driving forces behind Crete's economy. The warm climate and soil of Crete make it ideal for olive oil production, and Crete has between 30 and 40 million olive trees." My teammates and I were impressed by the perfectly aligned olive tree groves gracing the valleys and the mountainsides. Many orange and lemon trees also dotted the landscape.

Henry explained, "Crete can grow many different types of crops because it has several micro-climate areas that are specific for certain types of crops. Besides olives, Crete's crops include apples, bananas, artichokes, tomatoes, rice, avocados, pineapples, lettuce, carrots, potatoes, cabbage, carobs, horseradish, nuts, and eggplant."

After traveling for about 15 miles, we began to see a few small villages in the distance near the bottom of steep rising mountains, whose tops were partially obscured with clouds. Matt said, "Wow, look how high those mountains are! I'm surprised that Crete is this mountainous." "Yes, those mountain tops are snow-capped from October through the end of June," said Henry. "The melting snow helps supplement Crete's groundwater and the rainwater that is collected in cisterns. Unlike the nearby island of Santorini, which has no natural source of drinking water, Crete has plenty of natural water sources for its agricultural economy. That's why you see so many olive trees. Olive groves cover one fourth of the island," explained Henry.

The road narrowed as we came to the first little village, Charakas. Donnie noticed it first and said, "Hey, look at that high-rising rock on the western edge of town." As we got closer, we could see the blue and white Greek flag flying from a flagpole on top of the high-rising rock. Henry said, "That rock is 114 feet high and there is a 14th century Venetian Fortress sitting on its top."

We followed the small one lane streets through Charakas before stopping at the little roadside market to get some foodstuff. Henry said, "We'd better stock up here because this is the closest supermarket to our cottage in Treis Ekklisies. It's only eight miles away, but we must cross the very high Asterousia mountain range to get there."

The little Charakas market was the first of many such markets we would visit in Crete. The villages on par were about 5 to 10 miles apart, each having its own market. When we walked in the door, we saw shopping carts consisting of plastic red baskets on wheels. We grabbed a basket and began shopping. On our left, we saw various boxes of root vegetables, which we picked over and placed in plastic bags to pay for later. On our right was a large cooler containing fruits and fragile vegetables. Further on we came across boxes of salted cod - fish that had been caught and heavily salted for preservation. One box contained 40 or 50 large five to six pound cod fish. Near the cod fish was a cooler full of dairy products such as butter, milk, cream cheese, and other cheeses native to the area. Towards the back of the little store was a small cubby hole with various trinkets needed for kitchens, such as spatulas, strainers, toothpicks, etc. Just past the cubby hole, we encountered a meat cooler that had recently butchered rabbits, chicken, and some pork, but no beef. Crete did not raise a lot of cattle. There were also various fish such as salmon, octopus, etc. Next, we came to a tall cabinet with various selections of oil and olives.

The entire store consisted of six rows of various products like crackers, cookies, laundry powder, and cleaning fluids. It was a hodgepodge of home goods all squeezed into the space of a 20' x 30' enclosure. All the produce is grown in Crete, and it goes by seasons. Summer is an incredibly productive growth cycle for the store.

After we had made our selections and paid for our groceries, we exited the store and loaded into the van. As I started the van forward, Henry said, "We're very close now to Treis Ekklisies. We'll be there in about 20 minutes." "20 minutes? It's only eight miles further according to the GPS!" exclaimed Matt. Henry said, "Just look at the squiggly lines on Waze and you'll see why it will take another 20 minutes. There are about 12 hairpin curves going up this side of the mountain and another 20 hairpin curves going down on the other side of the mountain."

Sure enough, as we headed out of town towards Treis Ekklisies, the road immediately began to zig-zag diagonally back and forth with hairpin curves as it ascended the steep Asterousia Mountains. As we got higher up the mountainside, the sight of the Messara Valley below and behind us against the backdrop of the surrounding four thousand foot mountaintops provided us with incredibly picturesque views. We could see for miles. Several small villages about eight miles apart were nestled around the valley and the symmetrical olive groves. Henry said, “Pull over Connor. I’ve got to get some photographs.” I found a spot and stopped the van. Everyone jumped out and took some pictures.

After we got back in the van and resumed our climb up the mountain, we began to see goats and sheep foraging and grazing, respectively, on the grass, brushwood, or shrubs covering the rocky mountainside. Occasionally the goats and sheep would be laying on the road to soak up the sun and the heat of the pavement. I had to slow down several times to let the goats and sheep cross the road.

The only structures we could see on the way up the mountain were occasional shed-like structures for the goats and sheep. We passed by the rocky Kofinas Range, the highest peak of the Asterousia Mountains, at 4,038 feet. As we topped the mountain, we saw a small one-room whitewashed chapel with a white cross on the front edge of its terracotta tiled roof. Just one half mile further, we saw another white one-room chapel. Then another one-half mile we saw a third white one-room chapel. Finally, another half mile down the road we passed the small town of Paranymfoi, which had two Greek Orthodox churches, but no grocery stores. John said, “They sure have a lot of churches. I wonder if the same Greek Orthodox Priest tends to all those churches.”

The road from Paranymfoi to Treis Ekklisies meandered through some olive groves, past another chapel by a cemetery, and through some very rocky terrain along the plateau for about a mile before it reached the crest of the mountain where we would start our descent. The road to Treis Ekklisies was not paved until 2017. The significance of this fact was not realized by my teammates and I until we started the descent down the steep mountain to Treis Ekklisies with its 20 hairpin curves!

Henry was the first to spot several bearded vultures soaring along the cliff sides on the thermal air currents. Henry said, "I'll have to come back up here after we've settled in to get some good closeup photographs." I had to keep gearing down the van to first gear to make the steep hairpin turns. We did not pass any cars coming up the mountain, but if we had, priority was to be given to the car coming up the hill. The views out over this part of the Mediterranean Sea, which is called the Libyan Sea, during our descent were gorgeous with the sunlight shimmering off the calm azure water. Matt said, "Wow, that view is something else. Blue water as far as I can see. I wonder if we can see the coast of North Africa in Libya?" "Probably not," said Henry, "the coast of Libya is 187 miles away from Crete."

At one point during the descent, the road narrowed so that only one car could pass. At another point, a rockslide had taken out a portion of the guardrail on the lower side of the road. Bill said, "Be careful Connor, I sure don't want to go over the cliff." On the third from the last hairpin curve, I had to stop the van for several sheep to mosey off the road. I beeped the horn a bit trying to hurry them up. At the second to last hairpin curve, I had to dodge several goats who were crossing the road and grazing on the shrubs and forbs. At the last curve we saw one of the commonplace mini-shrine mailboxes with a cross on the top. The road narrowed to one lane as we entered the upper part of the village. The village consisted of about 50 whitewashed, concrete cottages in the shape of sugar cubes lining the limited hillside spaces in the semi-circular harbor between the mountains.

Henry said, "There's the cottage on the left, the one with the shutters." I parked the van on the small pullover area in front of the cottage, leaving just enough room for a car to get by. Everybody quickly jumped out of the van, eager to stretch our legs. Henry retrieved the keys from the lockbox and opened the cottage door so we could move our luggage inside and choose our sleeping quarters.

The cottage was two stories high and had a great layout with four bedrooms, two bathrooms, two fireplaces, and two back porches with panoramic views of the Libyan Sea. The inside decor was attractive with several references to sailboats, seashells, and the little Greek Orthodox churches. The color of the bathroom tiles matched the deep blue surface of the Libyan Sea. Small hand painted rocks lined the fireplace mantel, and there was a three foot long wooden replica of a sailboat with a tall mast sitting along the wall. Everyone voiced their approval of our temporary living quarters. "Hey Henry, your mother sure owns a gem of a place, doesn't she?" bellowed Matt. "Yes, I spent some time in the summers over here growing up and I loved it," said Henry.

After we had settled in, I called Gillian to let her know that we had arrived in Treis Ekklisies. I couldn't call her before 2 pm due to the time difference. "Gillian, you wouldn't believe how peaceful and scenic it is here," I said. "I'm glad you made it safely," said Gillian. "Everything is fine here. So, enjoy those panoramic views and give me a call occasionally to let me know how it's going."

I went into the living room just in time to hear Blake say, "Let's walk down to the water's edge. I can't wait to see how warm the water is." We all agreed and started walking down the one lane street to the center of the village. We noticed that several cottages had a small boat parked beside them. As we reached the center of the village, the asphalt ended and the road became a dirt road down the Main Street of the village, which was only about 100 yards long. The asphalt picked up again going up the other hillside of the village. We turned toward the beach, which was about 150 feet away on our left, and walked past a sign that said "Treis Ekklisies (Three Churches)."

CHAPTER 20

THREE CHURCHES

The village was named after three Byzantine churches built in the 14th Century on top of larger early Christian basilicas. The main church is the Church of the Virgin Mary, which operated as a small monastery until the last monk died in 1955. It currently belongs to the Parish of the Three Churches, whose priest resides in the old abbot's house.

As we continued walking toward the beach, my teammates and I passed the Church of the Virgin Mary on our right and saw flags flying on two flagpoles in front of the church — one was the blue and white Greek flag, and the other one was a yellow flag that represents the symbol of the Greek Orthodox Church. The natural stone facing of the church was an ochre or mud yellow color. There was also a covered stone alcove outside the back of the chapel and a stone courtyard beside the church connecting to three small stone residences off to the side for priests or other church figures. A WWII memorial sign stood prominently out front that read, "This is the place from which, during the German Occupation, trapped British, Australian, an New Zealand soldiers, aided by Cretan resistance fighters, who struggled for freedom and dignity, escaped to the Middle East by submarines and other means."

The second church, St. George's Church, was about 150 feet away from the Church of the Virgin Mary, and back towards the cottage from which we had come. It was a one room chapel built out of stone like the stone used for the Church of the Virgin Mary, and it still had two remaining Roman columns out front. The third church was The Temple of the Lord Christ. It was a small single-aisle, whitewashed church situated right before the entrance of Treis Ekklisies.

My teammates and I reached the sandy beach, where very light whitecaps were rhythmically collapsing on the beach. In the summer season, we would have passed a few cars and seen a few small boats tied to the moorings. But since it was off-season, we had the beach all to ourselves. Blake ran to the water's edge, reached down and got his hand wet, and said, "It's a little chilly, but I could get used to it." The rest of the guys walked along the beach about a half mile, absorbing the warmth of the sun while admiring the sea and the surrounding mountains. Donnie said, "look at that rock face up there. It looks like a woman's face." Matt said, "It sure does."

Henry explained, "According to a local myth, there once was a woman whose husband went to war and never came back. She used to sit on the rock every day, waiting for him to return, until she finally prayed to God to turn her to stone so that she would stay forever there and witness his arrival. If you walk up the road coming into the village, you can look down at the water and see the face of her husband soldier rising out of the water about 30 feet from the shoreline."

We turned around and headed for the one cantina that was open. Bill said, "I want to try a shot of their traditional Raki drink. I've heard it is like drinking Moonshine." Henry said, "You better be careful Bill. Raki has a 40-50% alcohol content, and it burns your throat going down. You need to sip it slowly and accompany it with some food. It is a symbol of friendship and is served on almost every occasion in Crete. Refusing a glass of Raki can be offensive to Cretans." "Well, they'll get no refusal from me," snickered Bill.

The rest of the guys followed Henry and Bill to the Taverna O Gialos and sat down at an outside table under the shade of a tamarisk tree. Henry said, "I've tried Raki, I think I'll stick with a local EZA lager." Donnie ordered a Vergina Lager, a beer produced by a Greek-owned Macedonian Thrace Brewery. John said, "I think I'll have a red wine." Matt, Connor and Blake started looking over the menu. "Fresh Dorado fish, lamb chops, salad and fried zucchini, sounds delicious," said Blake. When we finished eating our delicious meal, Bill said, "Well, Yamas," and he took a big sip of his Raki. His eyes widened and he pointed to his throat while fanning his hand back and forth. "Wow, I could feel that going down all the way!" The rest of the guys laughed as we got up from our seats. "Leave it to Bill to brighten up our afternoon. He hasn't changed since high school when he always had to be the first to try new things," remarked Blake.

CHAPTER 21

LARGEST CAROB TREE FOREST IN EUROPE

We started walking back to our cottage, but at the first turn, Matt says, "Hey let's walk up the other side of the mountain and see what the view looks like from there. We need to walk off some calories after that big meal." My teammates and I agreed and started walking down the center of the village on the dirt road. We discovered why Main Street was dirt, rather than asphalt when we got to the end of the Main Street where the asphalt started up again. The large Ampas Gorge coming down from the steep Asterousia Mountains emptied out into the Main Street dirt road at that point. "I guess any asphalt down the center of town would wash out after every hard rain," said John.

We started up the hill and passed several nice cottages. The road turned hard right at the top of the hill where two more nice cottages sat on the edge of the overlook. At that point, the road reverted back into a dirt road. Our eyes followed the dirt road along the coastline as far as we could see. We saw a very nice and secluded beach, a couple of cottages and a few associated sheep or goat structures. We also saw the largest Carob tree forest in Europe. "Carob comes from the pods of a Mediterranean evergreen tree. Carob beans are naturally sweet chocolate substitutes high in fiber, antioxidants, and they are said to lower cholesterol levels. Dried carob fruit is traditionally eaten on the Jewish holiday of Tu Bishvat," explained Henry.

CHAPTER 22

ST. PAUL'S MONASTERY:

Henry continued, "As soon as we've explored our immediate area, we'll start hiking the designated hiking trails. See that steep 2,800 foot rock-faced mountain behind the Carob tree forest? Hiking Trail number 14 heads straight up the mountain to where it meets Trails 12 & 13 about halfway up the mountain. Trail 12 continues westward around the mountain parallel to the coast towards Koudoumas Monastery. Trail 13 continues eastward around the mountain a ways before turning up and going over the top of the mountain where there is a 14th century Venetian monastery called St. Paul's Monastery. About a mile past St. Paul's Monastery is the little village of Paranymfoi from which the asphalt road leads to Treis Ekklisies."

"Can you tell us a little about the history of St. Paul's Monastery?" asked John. Henry continued, "St. Paul's monastery has an interesting history. It helped to preserve Greek heritage during the Venetian suppression in the 14th century. The Venetians had outlawed the use of the Greek language or the study of Greek culture. Due in part to its remote location, the church thrived during its association with the important scholar monk, Joseph Filagris, who led the nearby

Monastery of the Three Hierarchs in Lousoudi. Filagris led a school for the study of philosophical and theological manuscripts, focusing on the works of Aristotle. His school is considered by some to be the first university in Greece. His meticulously copied manuscripts and commentaries were later found in libraries throughout Europe. St. Paul's monastery served as a hermitage until the mid-twentieth century. The monastery of the Three Hierarchs was located in 1992 by a journalist-author Nikos Psilakis."

CHAPTER 23

BACK PORCH MEMORIES

We walked back to our cottage and sat on the back porch for awhile drinking a beer, breathing in the fresh air, and looking out at the Libyan Sea. "Look, there is a big ship way out there," said Matt. "Quick, get the binoculars," I said. Bill handed the binoculars to me, and I hurriedly focused them on the large cargo ship and said, "It looks as if it has some containers stacked on deck, and it is moving very slowly." We each took turns focusing the binoculars on the ship. "This trip is going to be relaxing," said Bill.

My teammates and I then began to recall some of our escapades from our high school track team. John laughed as he said, "Remember how Coach Ganzowski would jog around the track every morning in his bright red hooded sweat suit." All the guys laughed, and Henry said, "Good ole Coach Ganzowski. After Bill and I finished our practice jumps, we would just lay on the high jump mat and watch that red hood bobbing up and down while he jogged around the track at that turtle like pace." "Did you ever hear him tell his stories about how vicious the Turk fighters were in World War II," asked Donnie. "Yes," I said, "he was funny the way he'd cut his eyes up to one side and jut his jaw out when he was describing the Turkish fighters' ruthlessness. But he was a tough old bird, and I wouldn't want to be caught in a dark alley in a fight against him," I added.

Donnie said, "Hey Henry, do you remember the time we joined the streakers over on Cumberland Avenue?" "How could I forget," said Henry. The stories continued until dark when we began to retire to our rooms. For room assignments, the guys paired up just like they had in high school. The two high jumpers, Henry and Bill, shared a room. Matt and Donnie, the two long-distance men, paired up in another room. Blake and I, being best friends, shared a room. That left John in a room by himself, but he didn't mind, since he liked to stay up late and read.

Before I turned the lights out, I began my blog about our trip to Crete. I liked describing my daily adventures and including several of the photos I had taken with my phone. I firmly believed in the adage that "a picture is worth a thousand words." My family and friends enjoyed reading about my travels.

CHAPTER 24

HIKE TO HELIPAD

The next morning at breakfast, Donnie said, "What are we going to do today?" "I think we should start by exploring the dirt road on the eastern side of this village. It'll loosen up our muscles and see how we're going to do as a group before we tackle these huge mountains behind us," said Henry. "That sounds good to me," Matt chimed in.

By 8:00 am we had eaten our breakfast, put on our hiking boots, and assimilated out in front of the cottage. I turned to the guys and said, "Alright guys, Henry will lead, since he is familiar with the area. Does everyone have their water jugs and hats?" Everybody answered in the affirmative and we fell in line behind Henry. The first half-mile was on an upwards slope and I could hear some of our group breathing hard. Several sheep were grazing on the hillside on our left as we went by, and we could hear their bleating.

We reached a fork in the road just past the fenced-in large waste containers, out of which several skinny feral cats scampered. The asphalt road continued ascending the mountain to our left back and forth with hairpin curves, but a dirt road veered off to our right staying 50 feet above and parallel to the water's edge. There was a sign on the right side of the road with a map of all the hiking trails in the area surrounding Treis Ekklisies. Henry said, "Before we leave Crete, we will have hiked all of those trails, but today we're going to go down this dirt road on our right." The sun was gleaming over the relatively calm water, contributing to the peacefulness of the morning. The continuity of the beach areas was intermittently broken by large boulders sitting at the water's edge. The water would splash up against and between the boulders, occasionally emitting an upward spray of water as if the water was being blasted out of a cannon.

Donnie, who was behind Henry, suddenly said, "Hey look down there. A fisherman is casting his line into the sea from the shore." Everyone turned to look at the sole fisherman, who looked as if he didn't have a care in the world that morning. Donnie said, "How did he get down there? I don't see a car." Just then, we rounded a curve and saw a secondary dirt road turn off about 500 feet from where we were. It descended to the beach, and the fisherman's car was parked on it about 200 feet up the road from where the fisherman was casting his line into the sea.

We continued down the dirt road and soon saw several adult and baby kid goats foraging on the hillside. I was busy looking at the telephone poles and lines to my left. Blake said, "Connor, what are you looking at?" I replied, "I've been wondering how the electric lines came into Treis Ekklisies. I couldn't tell if they came in from the east or west, but now I can see that the lines go over the mountains from this eastern side of the village." Blake said, "It's amazing that they could get those lines over those steep mountains."

We were hiking at a pretty good clip and enjoying the scenery, especially the vast Libyan Sea below on our right and the rugged coastline with the steep mountains periodically jutting down to the water's edge. We had gone about a mile and a half and had only seen two cottages. The dirt road ended at what looked like a helipad and a retaining wall that had "Heraklion Hiking Club" written on it in big letters. We could see no other road or house in the distance ahead of us. "Well, guys, this is where we turn around," said Henry, "Everybody ready for a water break?" We grabbed our water bottles and sat down to rest on some large rocks that were at the mouth of a very steep gorge going up the mountain.

After a brief resting period, we reversed our direction and started to hike back to the cottage. Matt said, "I don't see any seagulls. What is that about?" "The Mediterranean Sea is oligotrophic," explained Henry. "Have you noticed how blue the Mediterranean Sea is? That is because, on the surface, the 'Med' is a 'dead sea' with very little plankton life. It gives the blue transparency we like on a postcard, but marine life doesn't like it. Thus, The Med is very poor in pelagic fish and that is what seagulls like to eat." Donnie asked, "What are pelagic fish?" Henry responded, "Fish that are neither close to the bottom or near the shore."

We made it back to the cottage, changed into our swimming trunks, and walked down to the beach. The water temperature was a bit chilly at 75 degrees Fahrenheit, but it felt good after our hike. After we had cooled off, we laid on our beach towels under the sun until it was time to go up to the cottage for lunch. We ate sandwiches and devoured the delicious oranges we had bought from the little market in Charakas. The oranges still had little green stems on them, and they peeled so easily. I said, "These are the best oranges I have ever tasted. I'll never get used to the oranges I get back in the States again." "The bananas are great too," said Blake, "everything here must be organic."

After lunch, everyone disbursed to do their own thing for a couple of hours. Bill and Henry laid down for a nap. Matt and Donnie started googling things to do in Crete. John began reading from one of his religious books. Blake and I sat out on the back porch talking. "That hike was pretty easy," I said. "Do you think you're ready for a steep hike up that big mountain behind us?" Blake quickly answered, "Sure, it'll be fun!"

CHAPTER 25

HIKING TRAILS 13 + 14 TO PARANYMFOI

Around 3 pm, the guys congregated in the Kitchen area for snacks. "What's on our schedule for tomorrow?" asked John. Henry said, "I think we're ready for our first big hike on Trails 13 and 14 up the mountain behind us to St. Paul's monastery. So, get a good night's rest, we'll start at 8 am tomorrow. Make sure you have on appropriate hiking gear and enough water for a six-hour moderate-level hike where we will follow narrow rocky paths up and back down the 2,800 foot mountain. I'm taking my camera and hope to get some captivating shots. Now, I've got to take the van over to Pyrgos and meet my mom's niece Sophia. As a welcoming gesture typical of Greek hospitality, she has baked us a delicious Cretan specialty – baked green and red bell peppers stuffed with rice, grated tomatoes, and herbs. I'll be back in time for dinner."

When Henry returned, everyone thoroughly enjoyed the stuffed peppers and then retired for the night. At 8 am the next morning, we were excited and ready to go on our big hike. Henry was giving instructions, "We'll have to pay serious attention to the markers. There will be red and white painted marks on large rocks every 75 to 100 feet, but the trail doesn't always go in a straight line and some of the marks are easy to miss. We'll take short water breaks on the way up. It gets steep as we get near the top and there are no guardrails. So be careful. When we reach the top, we'll see St. Paul's monastery and the little dirt road beyond it which leads to the village of Paranymfoi about a mile away. From there we will continue to Ambas waterfalls and then reverse our path back down Trail 13 to Treis Ekklisies."

As we started off on our hike, Henry beguiled us with a little Greek mythology, "By the way, legend has it that the village of Paranymfoi got its name because the inhabitants used to worship nymphs, a female nature deity in Ancient Greek folklore. Because of their association with springs, they were often seen as having healing properties. Almost all nymphs were immortal. There were several subgroups of nymphs, including ash tree nymphs, oak tree nymphs, spring nymphs, etc."

It was a beautiful 60 degree sunny day. "What a great day for a hike," said Blake. Our hiking group followed the dirt road heading west from Treis Ekklisies, always with the Libyan Sea in our view on our left. We passed the last electrical pole but could see that the water source continued through the black PEX-like tubing running along the ground beside the road. We saw the last two cottages and a few small, penned-in structures and water barrels for goats.

We were soon going through the carob tree forest, where we passed a lot of foraging goats, whose tinker bells clanged as they moved around. The incline of the dirt road started to increase, and we saw a sign for hiking Trail 14 and Paranymfoi just before the road forked. We didn't see the red and white marker on the ground several yards inside the right fork, and we elected to take the left fork, which stayed parallel to the Sea.

After traveling about 500 feet along the left fork, I said, "It looks as if this road ends up there against those rust colored cliffs in the distance." We walked about another 100 feet and heard several dogs begin to bark up near the cliffs on our right. The dogs were guarding about 100 sheep that were assimilated in a group near what looked like a large cave opening. We had already noticed that all the mountains surrounding Treis Ekklisies had several cave openings in their facings, both large and small. Henry spoke up, "I think we took the wrong fork. We'd better go back to the Paranymfoi sign and take the right fork going up the hill."

We turned around and headed back. When we had gone about 50 feet, we saw a very small, reddish-brown baby goat lying on its side and struggling to get up. It was very skinny and weak. There was no sign of its mother anywhere. John said, "Should we help it up so it can go find its mother or should we carry it back down to where we saw the other goats?" It looked so pitiful trying to get up that I reached down and gently helped the little goat to its feet. The baby goat was so unsteady on its feet that it could barely walk. It walked tentatively and swayed back and forth like it was drunk. I noticed blood on my finger and realized that it must be from the umbilical cord when I had helped this newly born goat up. The guys were tempted to carry the little goat back to the goats that we had previously seen, but we thought it might get rejected. The little goat occasionally made a weak baaing sound. Bill said, "I think it'll have a better chance if it sticks around here and waits for its mother to return." The other guys agreed and reluctantly left the baby goat where it was, hoping that the mother would soon return.

We reached the fork in the road and turned on the right hand fork this time. After walking about 15 feet, we saw the partially hidden red and white markers. "Well, it looks like we're now on the right path," said Henry. After going another 200 feet, the painted rock markers suddenly veered off the road and started up the hill among the brushwood covered landscape. The trail at this point was not very clear and we had to keep our eyes focused on the larger rocks about 75 feet ahead of us. The painted rocks at that point sat among all the small brushwood patches and did not always stand out until we had walked some yards up the hill past the last marked rock. Henry and the rest of us had to continue casting our eyes in a 45 degree arc on either side because the painted rocks were not in a straight line. As we got higher up the mountainside, we could look back far below and make out the dim line of the trail, which we had been unable to discern on our way up.

The views of the Libyan Sea got better and better as we went higher up the mountainside. We could see Treis Ekklisies in the distance, and the carob tree forest began to look smaller and smaller. Henry turned and asked, "How's everybody doing?" "This isn't too bad," said Donnie as he gulped a drink of water from his water bottle. Henry said, "Don't get too confident. It gets steeper as we go up." Matt said, "I'm glad I have my hiking boots, it would be easy to sprain an ankle on these loose rocks with my regular tennis shoes." Bill and John, who were bringing up the rear, were complaining that they had not brought their walking sticks. Blake and I were trying to spot all the foraging goats. The goat pellet droppings were all around, but the sightings of the goats were getting scarcer as we reached the higher altitudes.

About halfway up the mountain, Trail 14 came to a white cross placed in the ground, which appeared to be some kind of memorial or burial marker. The trail then began to run parallel to the sea again in both directions. Henry decided to turn left, rather than right, because the trail going left looked as if it was used more frequently and it had a red and white marked stone about 75 feet ahead. We followed Henry and passed two or three more painted rocks before we came to a sign that said Trail 12. Henry took another look at the photo of the trail maps that he had on his phone. He then realized that Trail 14 must have turned right at the white cross. Henry explained his mistake and turned the guys around. "I hope we don't have too many more wrong turns to make," said Bill.

We reached the white cross and continued past it about 50 feet before we saw another marked stone. Only this time the stone was marked with green and white paint. There was also a trail sign that indicated that we were now on Trail 13, which Henry knew would take us all the way to the top of the mountain.

Trail 13 soon became harder to see. We came to a point where we couldn't tell if the trail continued around the mountain or turned up the mountain. Henry couldn't see a marker and said, "the trail looks more used going around the mountain." So, we continued around the mountain as the trail got closer to some cliffs. As we came around the front edge of the cliffs, we saw a large cave on the cliffside that was obviously a shelter area for goats. Someone had fenced off part of the opening and placed some food troughs in the cave for the goats. There were tons of goat droppings, but no sign of any goats or people.

Although the cave was an interesting sight, Henry and the guys realized that we had taken another wrong turn. We took a few pictures then retraced our steps to the place where we thought the trail might have turned up the mountain. We started up the mountain and soon saw another marked stone ahead of us. We were back on the correct trail.

The trail got steeper and began to go diagonally back and forth in a zig-zag fashion as it got nearer the top. I looked ahead and said,

"It looks like we'll cross the ridge pretty soon." We continued going up the trail, which narrowed to what looked like a final passage through some large rocks, around a corner, and over the ridge. Our exuberance quickly turned into disappointment as we went through the passage and saw another towering mountain looming ahead of us in the distance. It looked as if we had another 800 feet of elevation to climb. A couple of the guys groaned, so Henry called for a break.

As we were drinking from our water bottles and looking up in the sky, we saw a group of about 20 vultures circling on the wind currents off the cliffs. Henry was ecstatic and quickly started shooting some photographs with his camera. Bill said, "Henry lives for these moments! His close-up photographs are quite good." "I know. His photographs of eagles and other birds at Radnor Lake in Nashville are amazing," I said.

After Henry was satisfied with his photographs, we started up the trail again. Blake noticed a couple of the black PEX water tubes going along the mountainside and said, "How in the world did anybody get that continuous tubing up and over these steep mountains?" That was one mystery we were probably going to have to leave unanswered.

Another 30 minutes of the steepest climbing of the trail brought us to the summit of the last mountain. It had taken us three hours to make it to the top, but we felt a great sense of accomplishment - just like we felt in our old track days when we had established a personal record in our running or jumping event. We marveled at the view all the way down to the Libyan Sea as we caught our breath. "That is a sight to behold," exclaimed Blake. All the guys got plenty of photos.

A herd of goats was at the top of the mountain, and they skittered away from us as soon as we started down the dirt road towards St. Paul's monastery about 150 feet away. A sign with Greek lettering stood in front of the church, but I was unable to decipher it with

Google translate. It mentioned the name of the monastery was St. Paul's and it said something about "Greek patriots," but that is all that I could make out. More pictures were taken before we started off down the dirt road toward the little village of Paranymfoi about a mile away, where we would rest before we turned towards Ambas Falls.

The going was much easier and faster on the dirt road into Paranymfoi. It only took us 20 minutes to reach the village. We stopped for another water break and rest. Blake teased the others, "I wonder where the nymphs were."

We then set off across the plateau for the Ambas Falls about a half mile away. The Mousoulis stream collects water from the springs in Paranymfoi and Amygdalos plateau and transports it to the beach at Treis Ekklisies. The waterfall drops off abruptly for 145 meters and is one of the highest waterfalls in Greece. We saw a sign at the beginning of the path to the Ambas Falls that indicated that hikers were discouraged from hiking to the falls during the months of January and February because it was the nesting period for Bearded vultures. Happy that we would not be bothering the vultures in October, we proceeded on to the waterfall. When we reached the waterfall, we marveled at its height and took some amazing photos. After a brief rest and water break, we turned around and started our trip back to Trail 13 in order to descend the mountain to Treis Ekklisies.

The early part of our descent down the mountainside was the steepest and required that we follow a diagonal zig-zaw path. The exertion required by the hikers on our descent differed from our exertion on the ascent of the mountain. Overall, the descent was easier and faster without the heavy breathing that we had experienced coming up the mountain. However, we did experience more muscle strain in our hamstrings and calves when trying to slow our body down. I also noted that my knees and feet took more pounding on the way down.

Soaking in the magnificent views of the Libyan Sea all the way down, we reached the bottom in one hour's time. We then followed the dirt road about a mile back into Treis Ekklisies. Our legs were plenty tired when we traipsed the last few steps into our cottage, five hours after we had started out that morning. Henry said, "Well, that six mile hike was exhilarating. It sure tested our 'old' muscles, but I think we passed the test with flying colors!" Matt jumped up and said, "When do we start the next hike? I'm ready." I said, "Hold on, not so fast. Not all of us run eight miles every day, Matt. Let's see how our muscles feel tomorrow." Blake said, "I'm starving. Let's shower and have some dinner. We can figure out our next hike later."

CHAPTER 26

OLIVE GROVES AND FELLOW TRAVELERS

The hikers were a little slow getting up the next morning. At breakfast, Bill said, "Let's take it easy today and spend some time at the beach or maybe just relax and read a book." John quickly agreed, "Yes, my big toe is sore today. I think I was putting too much pressure on it during our descent down the mountain yesterday." Henry said, "OK, everyone does their own thing today. We have plenty of days left. We don't have to hike every day. There are plenty of things we can do - like visiting a farmers' market, visiting the hippie caves at Matala Beach, or visiting an olive grove farm. I'm saving the big 12 mile round trip hike to the Koudoumas Monastery for our last hike."

Donnie asked, "What do you see during a visit to an olive grove farm?" Henry answered, "There's an olive grove farm we can tour near Heraklion. Harvesting of the olives begins in mid to late October, so we should see some of the workers harvesting the olives. They lay a large green fabric mesh under the trees, then use a pole with rotating triangular points on its end to shake the olives off the branches and onto the mesh."

Henry continued, "There is usually a tour guide at these olive grove farms who will talk about the history of olive oil production in Crete, then walk us through the entire process of olive oil production in their factory, followed by a tasting session of various types of olive oil. The factory contains a machine that washes the olives and separates the leaves and stems from the olives. Then a 4,000 pound rotating stone grinds the olives to a pulp and extracts the oil through filtering sheets. Extra Virgin Olive Oil comes from the initial pressing of the pulp, uses no chemicals, and must contain less than 1% oleic acid. Lesser quality olive oils use hot water and/or chemicals to extract the oil, which destroys essential nutrients and minerals in the oil." Blake said, "That sounds very interesting. Sign me up for that tour."

Donnie said, "I'm going down to the beach. Who wants to join me?" Everyone, except John, agreed to go to the beach with Donnie. We grabbed our beach towels and headed down to the beach. After a short dip in the sea, we dried out on our towels under the sun. Bill jumped up and said, "I'm thirsty, let's get a beer from the cantina." The rest of the guys followed Bill over to the outside table under the awning made from palm tree branches. The waiter came over and took our order.

I overheard the four guys at the next table laughing and speaking English. I nudged Blake, "Hey, those guys at the next table sound like they're American." "I'll ask them," said Blake. "Hey, are you guys American?" asked Blake. The tall blonde-headed guy said, "Yea! I'm Cameron and this is Tommy, Greg, and Stuart and we're from South Carolina. "No kidding," said Blake. "I am from Clemson."

Blake made the introductions for his table and said, "We're staying in an AirBNB here in Treis Ekklisies and hope to get in some good hikes. Where are you guys staying and what kinds of activities are you doing while you're in this little paradise?" Cameron said, "We're staying at the South Crete Escapes and we're only here for a week. We've rented a boat, and a tour guide has been taking us up and down the coast. It's great fun and we've stopped at several beautiful beaches. Today, we stopped and explored the 14th century Koudoumas Monastery about six miles west of here. It was really fascinating, and the chancel was built inside a cave. They have a huge overnight celebration of the Assumption of the Virgin Mary on August 15th of every year and many people attend and camp out in tents on the beach for the night festivities."

Henry said, "Really? We plan a hike to the Koudoumas Monastery from here for our last big hike. We've already been on part of that trail before it branched off and went straight up and over the mountain to Paranymfoi." Cameron said, "I'm sure y'all will have a fun time doing that."

We sat around talking to our new American friends and drinking a few more beers until dark. My teammates and me then said goodnight and wished our new American friends more good boating adventures. Cameron and his crew said goodnight and said, "Maybe we'll see you some more while we're here."

CHAPTER 27

MURDER SUSPECTS

Bill, Donnie, and I sat out on the back porch for a couple of hours discussing the issues surrounding our investigation of Steve's death. Bill said, "I've talked to Steve's sister Susan, and she said that Steve and Sherry loved one another very much and got along great. Steve did have a $1,000,000 life insurance policy, but their lifestyle suggests that $1,000,000 wouldn't be enough incentive to commit murder. They just bought a $1,5000,000 house in Farragut with a mortgage of only $300,000. They have only one adult son, who is a successful real estate agent. Sherry drives a new Audi and Steve drove a Range Rover. Bottom line, I don't believe that Sherry killed Steve, but I will run some more financials on her anyway just to satisfy my professional duty."

"What did the autopsy find?" I asked. Donnie said, "My wife's friend Pam is a clerk for Knoxville Police. She told me that the Medical Examiner found traces of digitalis in Steve's system. Otherwise, Steve had no known heart issues. They're looking at Sherry as a suspect, but so far there's no indictment."

"Good, we still have some time to figure out who did this," said Bill, "Who do we know has a motive, besides Sherry?" "Well, there's

Mitch," I said. "He told me himself that Steve messed him over in their business partnership when Steve never paid him his share for half the company. Mitch seemed pretty upset about it and wasn't letting it go even though it happened years ago." Bill responded, "OK, I'll run some financials and see what Mitch's economic situation is. Connor, can you follow up with a call to Mitch? Try to find out if Mitch talked to Steve at the reunion. If Mitch didn't do it, maybe he knows somebody else who may have held a grudge against Steve."

"There is also Lydia," said Donnie. "I heard her yelling at Steve at the Reunion. Something about Bitcoin." "OK, I can look into her financials as well," said Bill. "I'll give Lydia a call and see if I can get any more information about what they were arguing about."

"Other than Mitch and Lydia, anyone at our reunion could have slipped digitalis into Steve's drink," said Bill. "Death from ingesting a high dose of digitalis can occur within 30 minutes. We need to look at The Foundry's video surveillance to see who was close enough to slip something into Steve's drink. I've asked my assistant Karen if she could go by The Foundry and get a copy of the video recording of their security cameras for the night of our reunion. Let's compare notes in a few days after we've done some more digging."

CHAPTER 28

MATALA BEACH

The next morning, I said, "I vote for going to Matala Beach today. I've read that the beach is very nice with very fine sand like Destin, Florida. Also, I'm dying to see the hippie caves where Joni Mitchell stayed in 1970. She wrote the song "Carey" from her Blue Album about her time at Matala Beach." Henry said, "That sounds like a good plan. It's only an hour and a half away, and we will get to drive through some great agricultural country in the heart of the Messara Valley." Everyone readily accepted the plan to visit Matala Beach.

We grabbed our hats, sunglasses, swimming suits, and beach towels and loaded up into the van. I started the van up the 20 hairpin turns that we needed to navigate as we climbed over the mountain. As we ascended the mountain, Blake pointed out all the boxes of beehives that were lined up in several areas. "Do you know how important those bees are to the pollination of crops?" asked Blake. He then proceeded to explain the many benefits of raising bees. We made it up and over the mountain while passing only two small pickup trucks.

I drove my teammates through Charakas and then turned left, rather than veering right like we would if we were going to Heraklion. We were passing through a fertile valley with many different crops besides the ubiquitous olive, orange, and lemon trees. Recently plowed fields were planted with cabbages, tomatoes, artichokes, potatoes, and eggplants. It was Saturday and we saw several tractors out on the roads being driven mostly by elderly Greek men. At one point, Matt said, "Look at that elderly Greek woman standing on the sidestep of the tractor and holding onto her elderly Greek husband as he drives the tractor down the road towards town." The tractor was traveling at a fairly good clip, and we were impressed with the elderly woman's strength and daring.

As we passed through the narrow streets of several small villages with names like Dionysi, Stavies, or Asimi, we saw several elderly Greek women dressed all in black, including a black head scarf, sweeping their porches or carrying bags of groceries home from the store. Henry said, "Traditionally, widows wear black as a sign of mourning for a period of three years or sometimes, for the rest of their lives. The Greek people are a proud, hardworking people, and everyone contributes to the welfare of their tight-knit community. As you can tell by the beautiful and centrally located Greek Orthodox churches in every village, the Greek Orthodox religion is very important to them."

Before reaching Matala, we made stops in the little towns of Angioi Deka and Sivas. In Angioi Deka, we stopped in a little cafe on the Main Street for coffee, hot chocolate, and some ham and cheese baguette sandwiches. We toured the 12th Century church called Angioi Deka, named for the ten saints who were murdered there in 250 A.D. by the Roman Emperor Decius during the Roman religious persecution of early Christians.

John then convinced the group to tour the nearby Roman ruins from the ancient town of Gortys, which had been the Roman capital of Crete in the first century BCE. The ruins included the Odeon (small Roman theater), the famous law Code of Gortyn inscribed on a stone wall, the Praetorium (Roman Governor's palace), Roman Baths, the Nymphaeum (a monumental fountain dedicated to water nymphs), the Temple of Pythian Apollo, and the Basilica of Saint Titus (the first Bishop of Crete).

We motored on to the town of Sivas, which had an interesting little group of shops in the center of town. There was a traditional Greek taverna called Vafis Aposperida, which featured a "traditional Greek kitchen," according to the sign out front. Beside it was a coffee shop with two tables on the small, uncovered, outside front porch. Two gray mustachioed elderly Greek men were sitting at one of the tables quietly murmuring while keenly observing everyone who passed by. It was a scene my teammates and I would see in almost every small village. Across the street from Vafis Aposperida were two Cretan cuisine restaurants, one called the Karalis Taverna, and the other one called Mt. Mo Taverna. The chalkboard sign outside Mt. Mo featured a menu that included artichokes with lemon, goat in red wine sauce, spicy chicken with honey, vine leaves stuffed with rice, fresh grilled Dorade, stuffed courgette flowers with feta cheese, lamb kleftiko, and vegetarian mousaka, which is eggplant without the usual ground meat. Beside Mt. Mo was yet another taverna called Sigelakis, which featured boiled snails, red peppers, artichokes, fried rabbit, and souvlaki, which consists of meat and vegetables grilled on a skewer.

My teammates and I also visited a butcher shop in Sivas. It had a large signboard on the wall listing the prices for lamb, suckling lamb, goat, suckling goat, chicken, pig, and cow. The very nice Greek lady waiting on us offered my teammates and I some fresh baked Greek cookies, which were delicious. Blake also bought a jar of Cretan honey made from thyme, herbs, and wildflowers.

After leaving Sivas, it was only a short drive to Matala Beach. I began seeing more evidence of a tourist oriented town. We passed a few restaurants and signs for vacation rentals before rounding a curve and coming upon the parking area for the sandy beach. We parked the car and immediately noticed the Neolithic caves cut out in the big rock face jutting out into the sea about 500 yards to the right of the beach. We got out and walked on the fine grainy sand. Donnie said, "This beach is different from the beach at Treis Ekklisies. There are no pebbles mixed with the sand. I can see why this is a desired beach for the tourists."

Matt said, "I'm going to explore the caves. Anybody want to join me?" My teammates and I followed Matt over to the little booth, paid the $2 Euro admission fee, and began to scale the rock face. We stopped and investigated each of the 20 or so cave openings. Bill said, "I thought there would be interconnecting passageways between the cave rooms, but each opening is its own separate room." I said, "Look at that stone bed. I can't believe Joni Mitchell could sleep on something like that." Henry said, "She was only 27 years old in 1970 when she stayed here."

Everyone got plenty of photos of the caves and the picturesque view of the Mediterranean Sea. As we walked back to the van, we passed a young man with his snorkeling gear and speargun, who was heading for the water. We wanted to visit Vahti beach a few miles south of Matala beach, so we loaded up the van. I drove south until the pavement gave out at the Odigitria Monastery, which was founded in the 14th century and still housed six monks. I followed the sign pointing to Vahti beach and turned onto the dirt road. However, the road became very rough and rocky after about a half mile. I said, "I'm going to turn back. This road is too rough, and we could get a flat tire." Everyone agreed, so I turned the van around and said, "We've had a good day, but I'd like to get back to Treis Ekklisies before dark. I don't relish the thought of going down those 20 steep hairpin curves in the dark."

Our GPS took us on a slightly different route back to Treis Ekklisies. We enjoyed seeing a few different villages like Moirés, Loures, and Pyrgos. I stopped at a local supermarket in Pyrgos where we picked up a few grocery items. We also stopped at a bakery for some bread, and as we were exiting the bakery, we heard someone calling Henry's name. Surprised, Henry turned around and saw an elderly Greek woman dressed in black coming towards him. Henry recognized his mother's niece Sophia and said, "Oh hello Sophia. I didn't expect to run into you today." Henry introduced her to the rest of us, and we all began to thank her for her delicious stuffed peppers. Henry said, "It's good to see you again. We're having a great time in Crete. I'll tell my mom that we saw you in Pyrgos." My teammates and I then returned to the van and headed for Treis Ekklisies.

We made it back to Treis Ekklisies before dark. Blake and I carried the groceries inside the cottage. Blake said, "I'm cooking spaghetti tonight for the group." "My favorite," I said.

CHAPTER 29

LATE NIGHT MUSINGS

After a good dinner, my teammates and I sat out on the porch talking into the night. I said, "I'm glad we planned this trip. It's nice to catch up with you guys. At our 20th reunion, everybody was still caught up with their careers, raising their families, and accumulating assets. After 50 years, it's a more relaxed atmosphere. It's not all about our careers anymore. Our kids have moved out and started their own lives. We've accumulated all that we want. In fact, we're trying to downsize and get rid of things. But the best part is the freedom of our time. We can do whatever we like if our health allows it. We can focus on our hobbies or traveling and take trips like this one. We had a good friendship in high school and I'm glad to see that you guys kept your good personalities and did well in the world. I mean nobody became President or a celebrity, but nobody ended up in jail, right?" Bill quickly raised his beer and said, "Hear, Hear." We all clinked our glasses and then returned to staring out at the full moon's reflection off the water.

Look, " said Donnie, "I can see the lights of a ship way out there." Everybody strained to see the small glimmering light in the distance.

It looked lonely out there all by itself in the dark sea. I wondered what the crew were doing and where they were headed. What a different life they must lead than me and my friends.

CHAPTER 30

TRAIL 15 HIKE

The next morning after breakfast, Matt said, "Guys, yesterday when we were returning from Pyrgos and coming down the mountainside to Treis Ekklisies, I saw a zig-zagging dirt trail going up from the helipad where we stopped on our first hike. I think we missed seeing that trail when we ended our first hike at the helipad. We ought to go back today and see if it is Trail 15." Everyone thought that was a good idea, so we donned our hiking gear and started out towards the helipad at 9 am.

When we reached the helipad, Donnie said, "There is the dirt road over there. I thought it just went up to the last cottage. Let's follow it and see." We followed it around the curve and up to the last cottage about 75 feet higher up the mountain. To our surprise, it kept going beyond the cottage. "I don't see a sign for Trail 15, but it looks like this road will lead us over the mountain, so let's follow it," said Henry. We started up the steep road which soon began to zig-zag up the mountain. It was another beautiful sunny day. We saw no cottages, but as we gained more elevation, the view of the seacoast and the several cavernous mountains jutting down to the water's edge continued to impress us.

The trail started leading around the side of the mountain and we passed a couple of holding areas for goats with long feeding troughs, but there was no human in sight. We came around a curve and spotted a lone whitewashed one room Greek Orthodox church with a cross on its terracotta tiled roof surrounded by evergreen trees obviously planted by whatever monks or dedicated persons had built the church. Being the only structure around, the scene was pretty in its isolation. The stunningly bright white color of the chapel stood out among the otherwise brown and barren surrounding landscape. The tall skinny evergreen trees seemed particularly special because they weren't seen anywhere else in that environment.

It looked as if no one was around the church and we started to open the black wrought iron entrance gate to get a closer look, but to our surprise, a small, old, silver pickup truck meandered slowly into view. A short dark haired young Greek man was driving the truck with a bed full of goat feed bags that he was bringing to fill up the feeding troughs we had seen along the way. I asked him, "Does this dirt road lead to Paranymfoi?" The driver spoke no English and at first shook his head like he didn't understand. I asked again, "To Paranymfoi," as I pointed up the road going up the mountain. This time, the young man shook his head up and down as if he meant yes. We felt a little better and continued up the hill as we watched the truck slowly lumber down the road in the direction from which we had come. The driver stopped and unloaded a couple of bags of goat feed at one trough. We began to suspect that maybe he had not understood what we were asking, but we thought we could stop him on his way back up and ask him again. Unfortunately, he went out of sight around a curve, and he never reappeared while we were hiking.

Having never traveled this road before, I began to suspect that the road was going too far around the mountain away from Treis Ekklisies, and it was taking longer to reach the top than I had anticipated. I wondered at what point we might have to turn around and go back to our starting point at the helipad. About that time, the road turned back towards the direction of Treis Ekklisies as it continued up the mountain, so we continued to follow it.

Along came a second silver pickup truck loaded with goat feed. We stopped the driver, another dark haired Greek man a little older than the first driver and asked him if we were going the right way. He shook his head as if he didn't understand. But this time, I got out my phone and used Google translate to ask my question. The man read the Greek translation and said, "Yes." He started to drive on, but I stopped him again and typed into Google translate, "How far is it to Paranymfoi? One kilometer?" The man shook his head and said, "Two kilometers." I knew that 2 kilometers was about 1.2 miles. As the man slowly drove on down the mountain, we felt a little more confident that we were headed in the right direction and that we could make it the rest of the way.

For not the first nor the last time, I soon discovered that the local Greek estimation of distances was nowhere near accurate! Their slow pace of life didn't require that they accurately measure distances. They would get there when they got there. Even the websites for the hiking trails seemed to state distances "as the crow flies," rather than how many feet one traveled. At any rate, my teammates and I walked what seemed to be another two miles, and the village of Paranymfoi was nowhere in sight.

The dirt road finally crossed over the top of the mountain, and we saw one cottage sitting in the middle of a large olive tree grove.

We were heading westward in the direction towards Paranymfoi, but it was still nowhere in sight. About 500 yards further, we came to a sign that pointed to Treis Ekklisies down another dirt road on our left. We thankfully took that road and walked about another mile before coming out on the main asphalt road that led to Treis Ekklisies. We were tired, and Henry said, "We better skip Paranymfoi, and just walk the asphalt road back to Treis Ekklisies. We're too tired to get lost on another trail." Everyone agreed and started off down the asphalt road towards Treis Ekklisies.

Just before we crossed the top of the mountain a little over a half mile away, we saw a sign along the left side of the road that said, "Trail 15." "Hey look, there's Trail 15. The dirt road must not have been Trail 15 after all. I bet it was the original dirt road that went to Treis Ekklisies before the new asphalt road was built in 2017," I said.

It took us an hour to trod back and forth down the 20 steep hairpin curves, but we stopped a few times to get pictures of the vultures flying overhead or the beehives lined up on the mountainside in a couple of places. We translated one road sign that said that the area was a wildlife refuge, and that hunting was prohibited. The views of the Libyan Sea while walking down the mountain continued to be enchanting. Our leg muscles were tired when we finally arrived back at the cottage. Blake said, "I just want to get something to eat and flop down on my bed." The rest of us were proud that we had made the entire hike, but we felt the same way that Blake did.

CHAPTER 31

WALKING FOOD TOUR IN HERAKLION

The next morning Henry got us up early and told us that he had signed us up for a walking food tasting tour in Heraklion. A local guide, Marguerite, would take us through the downtown cafes and shops, stopping at various points to taste Cretan delicacies or to browse through some of the shops. Everyone was excited about the opportunity to participate in this special Cretan experience.

I drove the guys into Heraklion and arrived at 9 am at the famous Venetian Morosini Fountain built in 1629 in the center of the downtown district. Marguerite, a dark haired 45ish aged woman standing about 5'3" greeted us warmly and started us on our adventure as if we were long lost friends. She was talkative and described all that we passed as we made our way among the downtown streets and shops along with the regular flow of Heraklion residents.

Marguerite first had us stop at a little outside cafe with small round tables where she spoke Greek to the waiter and ordered small cups of traditional Greek coffee or herbal tea, depending on the individual preferences of our group. Marguerite explained that the Greek coffee was very strong and should be sipped slowly before one reached the coffee grinds at the bottom of the cup. The herbal tea tasted of sage and camomile.

The next stop was at another outside cafe where we tasted a delicious Greek pastry called a bougatsa, which was filled with yellow custard and sprinkled on top with cinnamon. In between the next stop we wandered in and out of the many shops. One shop featured numerous items made out of olive tree wood, including wooden spoons, bowls, saltshakers, etc. Marguerite explained that the Cretans did not waste anything and would use the olive tree clippings to make these items. Several shops had scores of Greek Orthodox religious icons, typically a wooden placard featuring a painting of a solemn faced Greek Orthodox Priest wearing his Kalpaki cleric hat.

Marguerite stopped in one store that sold various herbs, jellies, and syrups. The local owner was very helpful and had us taste a shot of a special tea. Marguerite showed us the dark brown carob pod that contained seeds that Cretans chew as a chocolate substitute or to make it into Carob syrup used medicinally for coughs, sore throats, and osteoporosis. Blake bought some Carob syrup and herbs, but as he was paying, the owner reached under the counter and pulled out a homemade jar of citron jam and thrust it towards Blake and said, "You must take this also, it was homemade by my mother." Blake couldn't refuse, and the owner added it to his bill.

Marguerite led us to our third stop, another outside cafe from which we could view the pleasing wall fresco across the alley. We were served a traditional Greek Dakos salad, which consisted of a robust double-baked barley rusk covered with luscious tomatoes, crumbled mixture cheese and a drizzle of the best olive oil. Henry exclaimed, "This is delicious!"

Our final stop was at the Kipkop Restaurant, which had been in operation since 1925. The atmosphere was typically Greek and included a painting on the wall opposite to the group of a sword-wielding young Ottoman Janissary or soldier wearing a black turban. Marguerite described each item that was brought out. The meal included roasted eggplant yogurt, Cretan deviled eggs, sausage with mustard, mushy yellow peas, Tzatziki sauce, olives, tomatoes, cucumbers, and tender, tasty roasted pork. While we were experiencing the delights of this Cretan meal, a young boy about 12 years old came in from the street and serenaded us with his accordion. We rewarded him for his performance with a tip. After we finished, we thanked Marguerite for a memorable Cretan experience and went back to our van for the return trip to Treis Ekklisies.

CHAPTER 32

RULING OUT SUSPECTS

The next day turned out to be a day of rest and relaxation. Donnie and Matt got up early to try their hand at fishing from the beach in the area where they had previously seen a fisherman. They had bought some fishing gear during their last trip to Heraklion and were hoping to catch and cook for lunch fish common to southern Crete, like a Pandora, Red Mullet, Red Porgy, or Sea Bream.

John was reading in his room and sending an email to his wife Mary. "Mary," he wrote. "We've had a great time so far. The Cretan people are so hospitable. We can see the dark blue Libyan Sea from our cottage. We've taken some strenuous hikes up the steep mountains that have provided us with some incredible views. We've also visited several small churches and nearby villages, as well as the capital city of Heraklion, where we toured several cafes, shops, and restaurants. It's been fun to reconnect with the guys — they're still cut ups when they get together. We've got another big hike planned before we must leave. Hope you're doing well and that everything is going well with Minister Bob. Love you! John."

Bill, Henry, Blake, and I reconvened on the porch to discuss any new revelations in our investigation of Steve's death. Bill said, "I didn't find any evidence of infidelity by either Steve or Sherry, so that's one less reason for the police to suspect Sherry. And a further investigation into Steve and Sherry's finances showed a comfortable net worth with no big debts lingering about. I found no evidence of a gambling or drug problem with either Steve or Sherry. Everything from that perspective seems to confirm our previous belief in Sherry's innocence."

Bill continued, "I talked to Lydia on the phone. She explained that a couple of months ago Steve had convinced her to invest $100,000 in Bitcoin in order to reap a quick profit. Instead, the bottom fell out of the Bitcoin market, and she lost three-fourths of her investment. She had been berating Steve about his poor advice at the reunion. But she said that, although it was a lot of money to lose, she and her husband had plenty of money and she certainly would not have killed Steve. My investigation into their finances confirms that Lydia and her husband are comfortably situated. Lydia earns $200,000 a year and her husband makes a similar amount with his filming and entertainment business. Their nice house in West Knoxville is paid for and they have no big debts. At this point, I think we need to focus on another suspect."

Bill turned to Connor and said, "I investigated Mitch's finances and found that he's certainly not on as sure footing as Lydia or Sherry. He makes around $80,000 a year as a sales manager for his company, but he's been divorced and has not accumulated a lot of savings. He frequently posts small items for sale on Facebook. What did he say to you when you asked him about Steve's death?"

I shook my head and said, "Mitch was as surprised as any of us about Steve's death. He said that, although their friendship had suffered greatly from the way their business partnership had ended, he still cared about Steve and would never have meant any harm to come to him. When I asked him if he knew of anyone else who might have wanted to harm Steve, he could only think of one person who might have held a grudge against Steve.

CHAPTER 33

SCOTT ROSSMAN

"Mitch said that back in high school, during one of Steve and Sherry's break-ups in their Senior year, Steve had dated Scott Rossman's sister, Sylvia. Steve and Sylvia were hot and heavy for a few months and went to all the parties. Word around school was that Steve was experimenting with drugs and had encouraged Sylvia to try cocaine, to which she quickly developed a habit. When Sherry came back into the picture, Steve dropped Sylvia abruptly. Sylvia didn't take the breakup well and continued to spiral into the drug scene. She moved on to heroin and OD'ed a few months after Steve broke up with her. Scott confronted Steve after Sylvia's death and punches were thrown. It was really an unpleasant affair. Mitch said that Scott lives in Knoxville and was present at our reunion," I concluded.

Bill said, "Well, I better look into Scott Rossman. Karen said she obtained a copy of The Foundry's video surveillance tape yesterday and is reviewing it. I'll ask her to focus on Scott."

Donnie said, "Pam told my wife that the Police are backing off Sherry as a suspect, so an indictment doesn't sound likely." "That's good news," I said. "I'll relay that information to Sherry and ask her if Steve had mentioned anything about Scott."

CHAPTER 34

MYRTOS BEACH

The next morning, Henry gathered everyone together for breakfast and said, "The plan today is to drive over to the Southeast coast of Crete and check out Myrtos Beach. It's about an hour and a half drive, but it's supposed to be worth the trip." We hurried through our breakfast and loaded up the van for the trip to Myrtos. I drove the van over the now familiar zig-zag road over the mountain to Charakas and then turned east towards Pyrgos. We drove through the town on the narrow one-way street, passed the little park on the eastern side of town, and continued through the Messara Valley passing one olive grove after another.

About 20 minutes later, sitting amongst several olive groves, we saw a roadside taverna with a tractor out front. It was called "Croppers Coffee Spot." I pulled over to park the van and we went inside to get some coffee. Inside, there were about six Greek men sitting at the tables, talking, smoking, and watching a soccer game on the mounted TV on the wall. Three gray haired men were at one table and three other men were seated at individual tables, but the conversation was going across all tables. The atmosphere was friendly, and they all smiled at us and nodded their heads as my teammates and I entered. I walked over to the counter and asked for some coffee from the smiling middle aged Greek woman proprietor who apparently spoke little English. Using hand signs, the woman figured out that we wanted a large cup of coffee and proceeded to satisfy our order. I heard one of the men behind me say in a thick Greek accent, "Where are you going?" I turned around and saw the voice had come from a dark haired, heavy set, smiling 45ish Greek man holding a cigarette. I said, "We're going to Myrtos." The men all smiled again and nodded their heads in a friendly manner. Then I added, "We're staying at Treis Ekklisies." And the same gentleman, who obviously spoke little English, said, "Ah." And motioned with his hand going up and down like he understood that one must go up and over the mountain to get to Treis Ekklisies.

Henry was eyeing some croissants in the counter window, and he used Google translate to ask what filling was in the croissant. The woman said it had a cheese filling. Henry and Donnie each ordered one of the cheese filled croissants. We sat down at a couple of tables on the other side of the small but inviting room. As we turned our attention to the soccer game, a woman arrived with her young daughter, who looked to be about eight years old. The mother and daughter excitedly came through the side door and ran to the woman proprietor who was obviously the little girl's grandmother. The little girl was pointing at the glitter surrounding her eyes and was proudly speaking Greek to her grandmother, who had raised her eyebrows and looked impressed. The grandmother gave the little girl a great big hug and the girl then ran over to one of the gray-haired men, who was obviously her grandfather, and repeated the performance. The grandfather had a puzzled look on his face but soon smiled and gave his granddaughter a hug as well.

I couldn't help but share in the joy of this warm demonstration of the loving nature of the Greek people. When my teammates and I had finished our refreshments, we made sure to say "efcharisto," smile, and wave goodbye to everyone as we left. All the Greek men and women smiled warmly and waved goodbye. It had been another happy Greek encounter for our group.

I started the van moving again towards Myrtos. Soon we started going up another huge mountain. Apparently, it was common to have to cross a big mountain before one could reach a beach in Crete. As I drove the van over the summit of the mountain, we got another glorious Cretan view of the Mediterranean Sea, and we came upon a WWII memorial park with a Cretan Holocaust Museum. I stopped the van, and we all wandered over to the park, which had about 10 stone pillars lined up one after another leading to the main center statue of a fallen soldier mounted on a large obelisk-like stone pedestal. Each pillar was inscribed with about 20 names of Cretan soldiers who had been killed by the Germans during the WWII German occupation of Crete. It was just one more representation to my teammates and me about how deeply the Cretans still felt about the suffering they had endured during the war.

We then walked over to the museum, where the attendant on duty told us that it was not currently open. I was confused by the reference to holocaust in the name of the museum, so I asked the attendant if the museum was to honor Jewish victims or Cretan victims. The attendant said it was to honor Cretan victims. I had seen WWII monuments in several of the villages that we had visited in Crete, and by all accounts, the Cretan resistance fighters never stopped opposing the German invasion force. I had noted that numerous monasteries had been torched more than once for assisting the Cretan Resistance fighters and for helping trapped British and New Zealand soldiers escape their beaches by submarine.

We then drove down the other side of the mountain and entered the town of Myrtos. Several modern buildings, condos, and restaurants were arranged along the stone tiled promenade which paralleled the beach. Cafes had outside canvas covered seating areas with tables and a pleasurable view of the beach. The town had an upscale resort feeling to it. My teammates and I sat down at one outside cafe and ordered drinks and our choice of a variety of Greek and seafood items that included sardine, octopus, squid, shrimp saganaki, Durade, and pork or chicken souvlaki. When we finished our flavorful meal, we strolled along the beach for a while, soaking up the warmth of the sun and the cool breeze from the sea. It was around 3 pm, so we loaded up for the return trip to Treis Ekklisies to make it back before dark.

CHAPTER 35

POLITICAL MUSINGS

We arrived back at Treis Ekklisies around 4:30 pm. John and I went out on the back porch to sip our drinks and take in the view of the Libyan Sea. The conversation started drifting towards the current political climate in the United States.

I said, "I think our country has lost the dream of obtaining fairness for all American citizens. We are on a backward trek where rights are being lost, especially by women and minorities. Women have lost reproductive rights; minorities have lost voting rights via stricter voter ID laws, limited mail-in voting, and reduced polling places in minority-heavy areas; both women and minorities have lost the benefits of affirmative action initiatives via the 2023 U.S. Supreme Court case of Students for Fair Admissions v. Harvard; and book bans have restricted the discussion of LGBTQ issues. The conservative politicians want to take away the constitutional right to citizenship in the United States by birthright. The magnanimity of our society has stalled, and self interest has moved to the forefront."

John responded, "Wait a minute. I think the liberal granting of privileges to anybody and everybody in this country has run amok.

Times have changed and fairness demands a different approach. The Woke agenda has gone too far in giving preference to the rights of the minority ahead of the rights of the majority. Christians are being discriminated against. Illegal immigrants are invading our country, taking jobs away from legal Americans, and putting a strain on our governmental budgets by having access to many benefits like: WIC (the Special Supplemental Nutrition Program for Women, Infants, and Children), healthcare at Federally Qualified Health Centers, public education with free/reduced lunch, emergency Medicaid, and short-term access to shelters and soup kitchens in emergency situations. Something has to change in our government's approach."

I replied, "There is no compromise in our political discourse. Everybody thinks their way is the right and only way. Christians want to force Christianity on everyone else. Muslims want to force Islam on everyone else. The rich want policies to help them keep their wealth and pay less taxes. The poor want more government assistance. Oil companies want to drill more, and environmentalists want to stop them. Some political voices even advocate for the use of gerrymandering to achieve their points of view."

I continued, "Our government should take a practical approach to illegal immigration and accept those who are already here. Illegal immigrants contribute to the U.S. economy. In 2022, their spending power totaled more than $254 billion and they paid nearly $76 billion in taxes. Also, a practical approach to the 2nd Amendment would not allow ordinary citizens to have bump-stocks, AR-15's or AK-47's."

John said, "Well Connor, I think that our government should loosen federal regulations and spur the development of our fossil fuels to stimulate the economy and ease up inflationary pressures on ordinary Americans. And as regards to abortion, I'm a pro-life minister who is bound by my religious beliefs. However, I do agree with you about restricting gun rights in so far as the need for increased background checks and a ban on rapid fire weapons."

"Well John," I added, "I agree that we need better border control, and I agree that we should do all we can to extract our fossil fuels, while still encouraging solar, wind, and electric power. If you and I can agree on some issues, why can't our two major political parties do the same?"

"I don't know, but we'll just have to hope for a depolarization of our political climate," said John before we both went in for dinner. As we entered the cottage, Henry was telling the others that we were going to make the big hike to Koudoumas Monastery tomorrow.

CHAPTER 36

HIKING TRAIL 12 TO KOUDOUMAS MONASTERY

The next morning everyone arose at 7 am to eat breakfast and start our hike by 8 am. We would walk along the dirt road to the west of town towards the carob tree forest, where we would pick up Trail 14 and start up the mountain like we had when we hiked to Paranymfoi. About three-fourths of the way up the mountain, Trail 14 would intersect Trails 12 and 13 at the white cross, where my teammates and I would turn west on Trail 12. From there the trail would gradually ascend towards the top of the large mountain in the distance that blocked our view of the Koudoumas Monastery. Once we topped that mountain we would see the monastery about three miles away. The hike from Treis Ekklisies to Koudoumas was six miles one way, so we had our work cut out for us if we were going to make the round trip back to Treis Ekklisies before dark.

It was another beautiful, sunny day in southern Crete as my teammates and I started along the road to the carob tree forest. Everyone was in a chipper mood. Matt and Donnie were out in front, followed by Henry and me. Blake, Bill, and John were last. Matt said, "This is a perfect day for a hike." Donnie responded, "Yea, it kind of reminds me of our early morning cross-country runs on Cherokee Boulevard alongside the Tennessee River." We were all carrying backpacks that were stuffed with our sandwiches, candy bars, a first aid kit, light rain jacket, and a sweatshirt in case it got cooler in the windier high altitudes. Our water containers were attached to the carabiners hanging from our backpacks.

Blake and I were discussing some of our old football memories. I said, "Do you remember that time our Little League football team took a bus trip down to Melbourne, Florida to play the Melbourne Little League football team?" "Yes," said Blake. "We stayed with the parents of the players for the Melbourne team, and we got to visit Cape Canaveral while we were there." I responded, "I think we lost our game, but we sure did have a great time. I wonder who planned that trip?" Blake took a drink from his water bottle and said, "I'm not sure whether it was one of the coaches or one of the parents. We had some crazy coaches, didn't we? Remember that time we were in white uniforms and were playing a game at South High after a hard rain. The field was all muddy, so the first thing Coach Sam made us do before the game was to run and slide down in the mud and get our uniforms all dirty. Coach Sam said, 'This way you won't worry about getting your pretty white uniforms dirty." I said, "Yes, it seems a little extreme now, but at the time it was fun, and we were all laughing."

About that time, we came upon a group of goats across the road. The goats quickly scattered as we drew closer, and we were subjected to a cacophony of goat tinker bells. Henry spotted the turnoff for Trail 14 as it started up the mountain and led us along the trail. Before long, the trail got steeper and John said, "I don't remember the trail being this steep this early. I'm already feeling it in my legs." Bill, who was beginning to breathe a little harder, said, "Yes, I'm ready for a short rest." So, we stopped for a break and Henry focused his camera on a few straggling goats in the large rock crevices up ahead and began snapping photographs.

After a short rest, we had regained our energy and started up the mountain again. The rocky path narrowed and began to zig-zag back and forth to lessen the incline as we went up the mountainside. When we reached the white cross, we turned west on Trail 12, and the incline of the path lessened for about 100 yards before it gradually started getting steeper again. Most of the red and white painted rocks were noticeable every 75 feet in front of us, but two or three of the markers were obscured until we came right up to them. At some points on the trail, the path was totally covered by gray colored rocks about five inches in diameter that had fallen as a group from a steep gorge above us. It was easy to lose the trail in those spots, and the uneven and sharp points of the rocks were tough on the soles of our feet.

At one point I looked back towards Treis Ekklisies, which I could just see sitting on the water's edge behind one of the mountain ridges that stopped short of the water. I saw a lone small boat motoring into the harbor of Treis Ekklisies and figured it was someone arriving for the 9 am Sunday Divine Liturgy at the Church of the Virgin Mary. I thought to myself, "The solitary nature of that little boat on the deep blue Libyan Sea would provide an exceptional scene for a painting."

The trail began to curve around one of the jutting mountains and head towards the sea on our left. Henry led us up the trail and over the top of the ridge where we could see another mountain range in the distance. The trail turned back from the sea and started following the other side of the mountain we had just crossed. The path continued inward in a large semicircular track towards the next mountain in the distance that again jutted out to the sea. As we started around the semicircle, Henry spotted three vultures circling on the wind currents arising from the rocky cliffs on our right. He quickly zoomed his camera in for a few shots.

We had covered about three miles since we had left Treis Ekklisies by the time we reached the next mountain crossing. Another white cross was sitting on the edge of the trail overlooking the vast Libyan Sea far below. We stopped for a water break. It was 10 am and Henry said, "We should be about halfway there. How is everybody holding up?" Everyone indicated that they were doing fine. "OK, if we keep this pace up, we should make it to the monastery around noon," said Henry as he started us moving again.

The trail leveled off onto a plateau of sorts for about 200 feet. When we had covered the 200 feet, the path started on a downward incline, and we could see that it intersected with a dirt road about a mile away. I said, "Look, you can see a little town way down there by the sea in a small harbor. I wonder if that is the Koudoumas Monastery?" Henry was hoping it was because he had only allotted three hours for the hike to Koudoumas Monastery, another three hours for the return trip back, and an hour for a visit to the monastery. He knew that he had to get us back before dark because it would be too dangerous on the rocky mountainous trail in the dark. We picked up our pace and soon reached the road, where we stopped for a water break at the small mud-colored one room Greek church sitting beside the road there.

Just then, I saw a small red pickup truck coming up the zig-zagging dirt road. I flagged it to a stop and asked the Greek driver, "Is that Koudoumas Monastery down there?" The driver said, "Yes," and drove on. We became excited and Donnie asked, "How far do you think it is to walk down that zig-zagging dirt road to the monastery?" I thought it looked like it was about a mile, but 45 minutes later as we trudged to the front gate of the monastery, I realized that distances can be deceiving, especially when viewed from an elevated perch and when the road frequently doubles back on itself as one descends the mountain.

We had passed several goats and a lone goat herder on what must have been a two mile descent down the road to the monastery. Our legs were thoroughly tired when we finally reached the monastery gate, and I was hoping that we would be rested and energetic enough to make the return trip after our visit to the monastery.

To our surprise, there were about six or seven cars parked outside the gate of the monastery. I had expected to see only two or three small trucks at this remote location, especially since any car would have had to travel 24 km over the dirt road coming from the village of Sternes on the other side of the Asterousia Mountains. The dirt road, which could get rough in places, was the only accessible road to Koudoumas Monastery. The explanation became apparent after we went through the large door to the stone-tiled courtyard and saw the Greek Orthodox Priest performing the Sunday service for about ten people, each of whom would light two candles and place them in the candle station outside the door before entering the chapel. We had unwittingly arrived just in time for the Sunday service. If it had been on a weekday, there probably would have been only two or three vehicles at the monastery.

On the left side of the church were three residential quarters, which the monks would graciously make available for overnight stays by visitors to the monastery upon request. The courtyard on the other side of the church contained a few picnic tables sitting under the shade of a couple of Tamarisk Evergreen trees which were enclosed by a stone wall surrounding the entire courtyard and church. The stone wall had windows that offered a view of the Libyan Sea about 150 feet away.

My teammates and I went over to the shady picnic tables and plopped down to rest our tired legs and eat our sandwiches. There were four other Greek people, dressed in black or dark clothing, sitting and talking at another table about ten feet away under a different tree.

After we had eaten our lunch and rested our legs, we were ready to explore the grounds. I wanted to see the chancel that was built in a cave. We exited the courtyard and saw the cave on a hill above a separate lone-standing building in front of which sat three Greek gentlemen. We passed the Greek men and waved as we walked along the sidewalk leading up to the cave. We clambered up about 20 steps and peered inside the windows of the cave. A small room contained an altar carved out of the cave wall on top of which sat a light blue spread cloth, a gold chalice, and a couple of placards painted with a solemn Greek Orthodox priest. In front of the altar on one side was a pedestal topped with a gold round bowl for holy water. On the other side of the altar was a wooden pedestal with an octagonal top for resting a Bible or some other religious textbook. Three chairs sat off to the side of the altar. The entrance of the cave was affixed with a large wooden door. We took some photos and, having satisfied our curiosity, started back down the steps.

As we passed the Greek men, one of men said in a heavy accent, "Where are you from?" I said, "Tennessee." The Greek man smiled and said, "Oh, home of Jack Daniel's whiskey." I smiled and said, "Yes. We have hiked over from Treis Ekklisies to see the monastery." The Greek man asked, "How long did it take you?" "Three hours,"

I responded. Then the Greek man said, "You must come inside and enjoy the after Sunday service meal with everybody." I tried to politely decline by saying, "Thank-you, but we have a long hike back and we must get started." The smiling Greek man insisted and placed his arm on my shoulder shepherding me along into the building with the other hikers.

We entered the building and saw three 30 foot tables arranged neatly on one side opposite the kitchen area. The tables were covered with tablecloths, and plates filled with food were already set out at each seat. The Greek man ushered us into some seats at the first table. About 30 Greek men, women, and children entered the room and took their seats. Five minutes later everyone stood when the three priests walked in and sat at their separate table on the side and said the prayer.

I was seated beside a bright-eyed young girl with her parents. I looked at the heaping food in front of me with a little dread because I was not hungry after having eaten my sandwiches. But I knew I could not refuse the warm Greek hospitality. I sat opposite to a middle-aged Greek couple and a white-haired man who was obviously a father to either the husband or the wife. Everyone smiled and nodded at me as I made my best effort to attack the huge serving of chicken, pork, and potatoes that was in front of me.

The original Greek man who had ushered our group into the building apparently was one of the organizers of the meal and kept coming over to see if we had everything we needed. He made a big production of bringing out a special dish of four dolmades that he placed in front of me and insisted that I try. I didn't know what I was trying at the time, but it looked like a big shrimp wrapped in some kind of leaf. My stomach was so full, so I started to cut one of the dolmades in half. The Greek organizer and the woman across from me simultaneously said, "No! No! You must eat it all at once." I held my breath and put one whole dolmade in my mouth. It filled my entire mouth cavity and almost choked me. My eyes watered, but I managed to slowly chew and swallow it. Everyone was looking at me expectantly for my judgment on this special Greek delicacy. The Greek man asked me, "Did you like it?" I nodded my head and tried to smile as I said, "Yes." The Greek man raised his hand and made a gesture of opening his four fingers away from his thumb and saying, "You eat the whole dolmade so that the flavors fill your entire palate. Have another one." This time I felt that I could politely decline.

When we had finished eating, we thanked the Greek gentleman profusely. The Greek man said, "See I offer you Greek hospitality and maybe if I come to America, you can return the favor!" We agreed and then slowly filed out of the building. The unplanned Sunday lunch had delayed our departure by thirty or forty minutes, but we felt we could still make it back before dark. I sensed that I had the stamina to make it back to Treis Ekklisies once I got on the trail, but I was dreading the two mile hike up the winding dirt road to the Trail 12 turnoff heading towards Treis Ekklisies.

We had no other option, so we started up the dirt road. We had only completed a couple of hairpin curves before a new four door Ford truck stopped and the Greek family inside asked if we wanted a ride. A man and his wife sat in the front seat and their three children sat in the back. Only the teenage daughter could speak English. I thanked them and said that we would be very grateful for a ride up to the Trail 12 turnoff. So, we hopped in the back of the pickup and rode up to the Trail 12 turnoff. We thanked the Greek family once more and started off on our eastward return trip to Treis Ekklisies.

The hike back to Tries Ekklisies was not as strenuous because the truck ride had shaved off two miles of our journey and saved us the energy it would have taken to ascend the 2,000 feet of elevation to the Trail 12 turnoff. As we hiked along the mountain range, we took some great pictures with our phones of the wondrous views of the Libyan Sea. When we got above the carob tree forest, the trail started its downward descent to the dirt road which led back to Treis Ekklisies. The hardest part was the last half mile on the dirt road going into Treis Ekklisies when our leg muscles had almost reached their maximum level of exertion. My fellow hikers and I flopped down on our beds when we entered the cottage and were down for the count for the rest of the evening.

CHAPTER 37

CHANIA AND RETHYMNO

The next morning, everyone slept in. When we slowly got out of bed, we decided that we would have a day of rest to recuperate from our long hike the previous day. Everyone lounged around the cottage taking turns washing their clothes, organizing their stuff, or calling their loved ones back home. Henry and I made a quick trip over the mountain to Charakas that afternoon to get some food items at the store. That evening Henry and I planned our adventure for the next day. We would drive over to the northwest coast of Crete and visit Chania and Rethymno, Crete's second and third largest cities, respectively.

I pulled the van away from the cottage at 8 am the next morning. We Cretan adventurers were looking forward to reentering the civilization of two larger cities. It took us an hour and a half to cross the picturesque Messara Valley and arrive at Rethymno on the northern coast of Crete. More houses and businesses began to appear on the outskirts of the city. As we drove through town on our way to the broad sidewalk promenade stretching along the coastline road, we began to see a younger crowd strolling the sidewalks and hanging out at small cafes. Rethymno was the official seat for the University of

Crete, but the University also had a campus in Heraklion as well. The Gallos campus in Rethymno contained the Schools of Philosophy, Education, Social, Economic, and Political Sciences. Obviously, my teammates and I were seeing several students at the University out and about. I stopped the van at the highly recommended Othonas Taverna where our group enjoyed another delightful Mediterranean lunch with feta and fig and great mezes.

After lunch, my teammates and I drove to the western edge of Rethymno to the hill of Paleokastro where we visited the Fortezza fortress, a large Venetian fortress built from 1573 to 1580 after the Ottoman pirate Ulrich Ali destroyed Rethymno in 1571. The fortress consisted of four main semibastions on the southern and eastern side (St. Nicholas, St. Paul, St. Elias, and St. Lucas) and three main ledges on the western and northern part (Holy Spirit, St. Justine, and St. Sozon). The grounds contained St. Catherine's Church, the Counselor's residence, several warehouses for artillery and gunpowder, and the Sultan Ibrahim Khan Mosque, which was built on the site of St. Nicholas Cathedral after its demolishment when the Fortress surrendered to the Ottomans in 1646 after a two month siege.

After my teammates and I had satisfied our historical curiosity about the Fortezza Fortress in Rethymno, we loaded in the van and headed west along the northern coastline on Greek National Highway 90 for the one hour drive to Chania, the 4,000 year old city that has been called "the Venice of the East." As I drove along, I said, "I read that they filmed 'Zorba the Greek' in Chania."

We drove into Chania, parked the van, and strolled through the large downtown open market area with its many vendors. Afterwards, we drove the van towards the harbor and found parking just outside the old Venetian Harbor. My teammates and I walked along the wide stone-tiled promenade in the semicircular harbor perusing the occasional vendor who had set up tables to display their wares, as well as, the several restaurants, cafes, and shops. We stopped for coffee and bougatsa at one of the outside cafes while we admired the large Chania lighthouse at the end of the pier on the other side of the harbor.

My teammates and I continued around the harbor and stopped to watch a film crew shoot a classically Greek scene on the promenade with the Cretan Sea as a backdrop. The director had 20 Greek actors dressed uniformly in Greek warrior or noble costumes of the Ottoman era lined up as if they were marching. The 10 slender women wore white skirts covering white pants, black shoes, a red belt with a flowing red apron down behind, a short black bolero jacket, and a tall red fez with an attached red scarf flowing down the back. The 10 Greek men wore white long sleeved shirts covered by mid-thigh royal blue vests, a wide brown belt housing a small sword in front, tight black pants tucked into knee-high white boots, and black hats. My teammates and I quickly got out our phones and took some photographs.

We finished our visit to Chania by shopping in a couple of the stores on the promenade. I purchased a beautiful Saraki scarf for Gillian. It had been a pleasant visit to Chania, but we had to start the return trip to Treis Ekklisies to arrive before dark. The drive back was relatively uneventful, and we discussed all that we had seen for that day.

CHAPTER 38

GOODBYE TO TREIS EKKLISIES

The next day would be our last day in Treis Ekklisies and we would need to pack up for our return trip home, which would include the ferry ride from Heraklion to Athens, and then a RyanAir flight to Naples for a visit to Italy for a few days before we flew back to the United States.

We woke up the next morning at 8 am to straighten up the cottage and pack our luggage. "It's been a great visit to Crete," I told Henry. "I never would have been able to appreciate the beauty of Crete without this trip. Spending time with and hiking with old friends has been a big pleasure. You must thank your mother and tell her what a great adventure this has been." Henry responded, "I will do that. I too am glad to have spent this time with old friends in such a beautiful place."

Matt said, "I'm going down to the beach one more time before we leave. Who will join me?" Henry, John, and Blake got up and accompanied Matt to the beach. Bill, Donnie, and I went out on the back porch for another discussion of our murder investigation. Bill spoke first, "Karen reviewed The Foundry's security camera footage on the night that Steve was killed, and she saw several classmates who were close enough to Steve to have put something in his drink, including Scott Rossman. At this point, I think we should focus on Scott, since we suspect that he could have a motive. I'll do some research and see what his situation is."

Donnie and the other guys got back to the cottage in time for lunch. We ate our sandwiches and decided to take one last small hike up the road to the mini-shrine where we could get one last group photo with the Libyan Sea as a backdrop.

We started up the road glancing out at the Libyan Sea the entire way. There was something calming about looking out across the shimmering blue water as far as one could see until the sea blended into the blue sky on the horizon. I was really going to miss this view. A slight breeze ruffled my hair as we walked along the road gaining altitude as we went. By the time we reached the mini-shrine, we were about 200 feet higher than the Libyan Sea. Henry set his camera on a large rock and had us all line up side by side with the Libyan Sea behind us. He focused his lens, set the automatic timer, and ran over to us so he would be in the picture too. We heard the camera snap three times. Henry rushed back over and looked at the digital pictures before giving us a thumbs up. We then reversed our path and headed back to the cottage.

When we reached the cottage, Henry ran back in to make sure no one had left anything. A couple of minutes later he exited the front door and locked it behind him. We all climbed into the van, and I started the van up the road as we climbed the mountain for the last time.

SOLVING THE MURDER

CHAPTER 39

FERRY BACK TO ATHENS

An hour and a half later, we pulled up to the Heraklion Pier, where I let the guys off with our luggage. They were going to wait in the cafe while I returned the van to the car rental agency at the airport. I would return to the Pier in a taxi. Our ferry didn't depart until 9 pm, so we planned to store our luggage in the cafe and make another quick visit to the Heraklion downtown district.

I returned the van and made it back to the Pier in 45 minutes. I joined my teammates in the cafe, where they shared their opinions on what they liked most about Crete. We grabbed a couple of taxis for the downtown district. After the taxis let us off, we stopped in a cafe for another tasty bougatsa before we meandered in and out of the shops looking for gifts to bring back to our loved ones in the States. I bought a set of spatulas made of olive tree wood for Gillian. She loved cooking and would appreciate the wooden spatulas.

The time passed quickly and before we knew it, it was time to head back to the Pier. We pulled our luggage over to the line that had formed in front of the ferry. We heard a whistle blow and saw the line start moving up the boarding plank to the ferry. Within 15 minutes, we were comfortably seated in our assigned "airplane" seats for the nine hour sea crossing to Athens.

CHAPTER 40

SCOTT ROSSMAN'S DENIAL

About two hours into the ferry ride, Bill got a call from his assistant Karen about her investigation of Scott Rossman. He listened for about ten minutes and then thanked her before hanging up. "What did she say?" I asked. Bill began, "It turns out that Scott is a botanist, who would have easy access to digitalis. He lost his mother in June and his wife in July of this year, both to cancer. His work supervisor said that he has been under a lot of stress dealing with his dying mother and wife. He has missed a lot of work during the past year, and he has no children or family to help him cope with his grief. His supervisor had to write him up a couple of times for violent outbursts. His coworkers said that he had talked a lot about his upcoming reunion and had said that some of his classmates were jerks. He mentioned more than once that he had lost his only sister to a drug overdose that started in high school. Finally, Scott is seen on the security camera stopping by Steve's table while Steve had gone to the restroom. The view is partially obscured, but it looks like Scott may have dropped something in Steve's glass when he got up."

"We need to get this information to the police as soon as we can," I said. Bill nodded and said, "I know. I told Karen to get in touch with the police detective tomorrow. I'm going to call Scott and see how he reacts to my questions."

Bill called the number that Karen had given him. "Hello," said Scott. "Hello, Scott. This is Bill Boyer from your West High School class. I'm a private investigator and I'm calling all of our Saturday night reunion attendees to see if they saw anything in regards to Steve's death. Do you mind if I ask you a few questions?" "No, I don't mind. I was there, but I left before Steve collapsed. I heard that the police think that he was poisoned." "Yes, that's right. The Medical Examiner found high levels of digitalis in his bloodstream." "Do the police have any suspects yet?" "No, they're still in the early phases of their investigation. Scott, did you happen to talk to Steve at any point during the evening?" "No, I didn't get the chance." "Did you happen to see anyone congregating around his table who might have been close enough to slip a lethal dose of digitalis in Steve's drink?" "No."

Bill said, "We've reviewed the video surveillance tapes, and at one point you were seen sitting in Steve's seat talking to Ronnie Coker. Did you put anything in Steve's drink?" "No. I just stopped at his table for a few minutes to say hi to Ronnie." "You are a botanist, and you have access to digitalis in your work, right?" "Wait a minute. Are you accusing me of having something to do with Steve's death?" "Did you?" "I think I'm done talking to you. I have nothing more to say to you, Goodbye," said Scott as he hung up the phone.

Bill turned to me and said, "He sounded rattled. I'll call the police detective tomorrow and talk to him about what we know." "Do you think he's guilty?" I asked. "I'm liking him as the killer. I just don't know if we can prove it," said Bill.

Bill and I settled back into our chairs and eventually fell asleep with the rest of our teammates as the ferry plugged along throughout the night.

CHAPTER 41

ATHENS

The ferry arrived at Piraeus Port at 6:00 am. We were awakened by the loudspeaker announcing our arrival. I slowly got out of my seat and stretched my arms and legs, as did the rest of my teammates. We gathered our luggage and proceeded towards the exit where other passengers were already in a long line.

It took us about 15 minutes to get off the ferry. Our RyanAir flight to Naples did not leave until 4 pm, so we caught a taxi to the Acropolis. I had previously visited the Acropolis with Gillian five years earlier and was awed by the size and historical significance. Henry and Bill had also visited the Acropolis previously, but the rest of our teammates couldn't wait to tour the grounds. We first stored our luggage in some lockers and grabbed breakfast at one of the cafes at the bottom of the hill around the Acropolis.

John was most impressed during our tour of the Acropolis after breakfast. He kept saying, "Can you believe that these huge buildings were built by the Greek people over 400 years before Christ was born?" Everyone took a lot of pictures and enjoyed our visit.

After our tour, we visited some shops and then retrieved our luggage. We rode the Metro train to the airport, where we checked our bags and made our way to the food court to get some lunch.

After lunch we made our way to the RyanAir gate and found some seats.

The time passed quickly, and we began boarding at 3:30 pm. The flight was uneventful, and we touched down in Naples at 6 pm. We retrieved our luggage and took a taxi to our AirBNB. We settled in and ordered pizza for dinner.

CHAPTER 42

DETECTIVE ADAM PETROSKEY

After dinner, Bill called Detective Adam Petrosky with the Knoxville Police Department and explained our findings. "We really think he is the murderer," said Bill. "He had a motive, access to digitalis as a botanist, and the video surveillance shows that he was physically seated at Steve's table for a short period of time." Detective Petroskey responded, "Yes, I've seen the video tape. Your assistant Karen brought it by this morning. I've asked Scott to come in for an interview today at 3 pm. Maybe, if we're lucky, we can get a confession." I replied, "Thanks Detective. He seemed rattled when Bill questioned him yesterday. The death of his mother and wife, so close together, may have put him over the edge."

Scott Rossman showed up at the West Knoxville Police Precinct at 2:50 pm with his attorney, Brian Williams. They were directed to the interview room, and Detective Petrosky entered a few minutes later. Introductions were made and Detective Petrosky said, "I'm investigating the murder of Steve Sanders on August 3, at your high school reunion at The Foundry, and I just want to ask you some questions." "OK," said Scott. "You were present at the reunion, correct?"

"Yes, but I left before Steve collapsed." "Did you see or talk to Steve at any time while you were at the Reunion?" "Well, yes I saw Steve, but I didn't speak to him." "What is your occupation Scott?" "I'm a Botanist for the University of Tennessee Agricultural Department." "So, you have access to many different kinds of plants in your job?" "Yes, that's right." "Would you have access to digitalis at your work or any other place?" Brian interjected, "You don't have to answer. My client invokes his Fifth Amendment right against self-incrimination and will not be answering that question." "Your only sister died of a drug overdose while she was at West High School, correct?" "Yes, that's correct." "You were very close to your sister, correct? "Yes." "Isn't it true that your sister dated Steve Sanders for a time at West High?" "Yes." "How would you describe the end of their relationship? Who broke off the relationship, Steve or your sister?" "Well, I'd say it was a mutual decision." "So, there were no hard feelings?" "Well, I think my sister took it harder than Steve did." "Did you know that Steve introduced your sister to cocaine use while they were dating?" "No, I had no firsthand knowledge of that." "But wasn't that common knowledge among your classmates at the time?" "I can't speak for them." "Did you know that your sister was going to a lot of parties with Steve?" "Well, I was aware that they were going out and that included going to the occasional party." "Are you aware of any drug use at those high school parties?" "Well, I think that there is probably always some drug use going on at a high school party." "Isn't it true that your sister took her break up with Steve very hard and spiraled into heavy drug use, which ultimately led to her OD'ing with heroin?" "My sister tried to break her addiction but just couldn't stop." "Do you blame Steve for introducing your sister to drug use?" "No." "Isn't it true that you believe your sister would still be alive today if it were not for Steve Sanders?" "No, that's not true." "The video surveillance of the night of your reunion shows you sitting down in Steve's seat for a period of time, while he had gone to the restroom. Isn't it true that you slipped a lethal dose of digitalis in Steve's glass while you were sitting in his seat?" "No, No. I just sat down to talk to Ronnie." Brian interjected, "I think my client has answered your questions to the best of his knowledge and has no further information to add. Unless you are prepared to charge him for a crime at this time, we are done for the day." "OK Scott, thank-you for coming in today. I'd recommend that you do not leave town. We may have some further questions for you."

Scott and Brian got up and left the police station. Brian told Scott, "Listen, they have no direct proof connecting you to Steve's death. Just sit tight and don't say anything to anybody about your actions at the reunion or your thoughts about Steve. And call me before you speak to Detective Petroskey or any other police. OK?" Scott said, "OK," but he looked worried when he left Brian.

CHAPTER 43

POMPEII AND AMALFI COAST

The evening that we arrived in Naples, Henry gathered everyone together and said, "OK guys, we're in for a treat tomorrow. I have rented a private tour bus to take us to Pompeii, where we will see the remains of the city that was destroyed by the volcanic eruption of Mt. Vesuvius in 79 AD. Afterwards, we'll then tour the Amalfi Coast, which is like a fairy-tale. So, get your rest. We head out at 7 am tomorrow."

We got up early the next morning and ate a quick breakfast. The tour bus for Pompeii arrived at our AirBNB right on time at 7 am. We boarded up and settled in for the 30 minute drive to Pompeii.

We could see Mt. Vesuvius hovering in the distance when we got to Pompeii. We proceeded to walk through the ancient Roman streets, passing the forum, the amphitheater, the brothel, the Stabian baths, the Villa of the Mysteries with its well preserved frescoes, and the House of the Faun with its famous Alexander the Great mosaic. Everyone, especially John, was impressed with the historical significance of the 1599 discovery of the buried Pompeii ruins by Dominico Fontana. We finished our visit with a short lunch.

Our tour bus then started on the hour long ride to the Amalfi Coast. As we approached the dramatic cliffs and coastal roads of the Amalfi Coast, our driver put on a CD of romantic Italian music, which made us more receptive for the amorous views to come. I was amazed at our driver's expert ability to negotiate the narrow winding streets as we entered the first coastal village of Sorrento. The views of the pastel colored buildings and the Tyrrhenian Sea below were stunning. We continued along the coastal drive to the next equally photogenic village of Positano, where we stopped to visit the small boutique shops. I purchased a decorative tile for Gillian.

Our last village before returning to Naples was Amalfi, the heart of the coast. We visited the Amalfi Cathedral and walked along the Piazza del Duomo, stopping at a cafe to try the famous drink, Limoncello. When we had taken our photos and gotten a nice feel for the village, it was time to return to our bus for the drive back to Naples.

We arrived back at our AirBNB in Naples just before dark. We thanked our tour guide with a generous tip and went inside. "Man, what a day," Blake said. "Yes," said Donnie. "I need to bring my wife back to the Amalfi Coast."

Henry said, "OK, guys, we have two more days before we fly back to Knoxville. We will catch the fast train early tomorrow morning for Rome, where we'll see the sights and stay overnight in another AirBNB that I have booked. Then we'll return to the Naples airport to catch our 8 pm United Airlines flight back to the U.S."

CHAPTER 44

ROME

The fast train ride to Rome the next morning took an hour and ten minutes and cost $40 Euros. We arrived around 8:30 am and headed for the Colosseum for our first photo opportunity. We then purchased tickets for the Hop-On-Hop-Off Bus tour, which took us around the city with an audio guide for all the sights. We made stops at St. Peter's Basilica and Vatican City, where we saw Michaelangelo's masterpiece in the Sistine Chapel. We wound up the evening by tossing a coin into the Trevi Fountain. It didn't take long for us to fall asleep in our AirBNB after our whirlwind day.

The next morning after breakfast, we toured the sights again from the Hop-On-Hop-Off Bus. We had lunch at the Taverna del Fori Imperiali where Blake and I savored the pasta dish, carbonara. It had been a short visit to Rome, but that is all we had planned. After lunch, we returned to the train station for our trip back to the Naples Airport.

CHAPTER 45

RETURN FLIGHT TO KNOXVILLE

We boarded our United Airlines flight at 7:30 pm, somewhat relieved that we were headed home. We couldn't have packed anything more on our trip to Crete. It was great to reconnect with the guys, but I was ready to return home to Gillian and my Nashville home.

Bill sat next to me on the flight home. We discussed our murder investigation. Bill said, "We need to give Detective Petroskey a call as soon as we get back." I replied, "Yes, I'm curious how his interview went with Scott." "Can you stay over in Knoxville for another day to join me on a visit to Detective Petroskey?" asked Bill. "Let me run it by Gillian, but I'm sure she won't mind," I said.

Our United Flight had stops and short layovers in Munich and Newark. We arrived in Knoxville around 4 pm. My teammates and I gave each other heartfelt goodbyes and promised to stay in touch before parting on our separate ways.

CHAPTER 46

MEETING WITH DETECTIVE PETROSKEY

I called Gillian and told her to wait a day before coming over to Knoxville to pick me up. Bill pulled me aside and said, "I'll pick you up from your hotel tomorrow morning at 9 am. I have arranged an appointment with detective Petrosky at 10 am at the West Knoxville Police precinct to discuss how the murder investigation is going." "Sounds good, I'll be ready," I said.

Bill picked me up from the Marriott Residence Inn near Cedar Bluff at 9 am sharp the next morning. We made a stop for donuts and coffee and arrived at Detective Petroskey's precinct 15 minutes early. Bill said hello to some of the old timers he knew as he entered the precinct. Detective Petroskey came out and greeted us. Bill said, "Here, have a donut." "Thanks! Come on back to my office," said Detective Petroskey. We followed him through the maze of desks in the front open area where about ten precinct workers were busy answering phones, rummaging through the files stacked on their desks, or entering data on their computer screens. Just past the main open area, Detective Petroskey entered a glass door to his office on the right and said, "Have a seat."

Bill and I sat down in a couple of chairs facing Detective Petroskey's desk. Bill asked, "Did you get a chance to interview Scott?" Detective Petroskey said, "Yes, I interviewed him yesterday, and I think he's our man. He had his lawyer with him, so I didn't get him to admit anything. But he appeared fidgety, and I think he was lying to me with his answers. He admitted to sitting in Steve's seat briefly, but he denied putting anything in Steve's drink. Without a corroborating witness who saw Scott put the digitalis in Steve's drink, we have a very high burden to climb to get the DA to charge Scott. I don't think a jury would convict Scott on the circumstantial evidence that we have."

I turned to Bill and said, "We've got to talk to Ronnie and see if he saw anything. We can't let Scott get away with this." Bill asked Detective Petroskey, "What about Scott's co-workers? Can you question them to see if they know anything about Scott working with digitalis?" "I'm following up with his co-workers. It would still be a long shot even if they confirmed that Scott was working with digitalis. They would not have seen Scott at the reunion. We'd be in better shape if the video surveillance had clearly shown Scott placing something in Steve's drink," said Detective Petroskey.

Bill said, "Well, Connor and I appreciate everything you're doing on this case. Steve's wife Sherry has been very upset and worried about the whole affair. Has Sherry been eliminated as a suspect?" Detective Petroskey responded, "Tell her not to worry. By all accounts she and Steve were happily married. There's nothing to indicate that she wanted him dead, needed the life insurance money, or had access to digitalis. Scott is our primary suspect at this point."

"Thanks Detective Petroskey," I said. Bill and I got up to leave and Bill asked Detective Petroskey, "Will you let us know if you make any progress?" "Sure thing. Thanks for coming in," said Detective Petroskey as he stood and shook our hands.

As Bill and I left the building, Bill said, "I'm going to give Ronnie a call right now." Bill found Ronnie's number and punched it on his cell phone. "Hello," answered Ronnie. "Hello Ronnie, this is Bill Boyer and I'm here with Connor Stuart. We're investigating the death of Steve Sanders, and we wanted to know if we could ask you a few questions." "Sure, how can I help." "You were sitting at Steve's table, weren't you?" "Yes. It was really frightening when he just collapsed. We didn't know what happened." "Earlier in the evening before Steve collapsed, did Scott Rossman come over to the table, sit down, and talk to you for a few minutes." "Yes, he did. I had not seen him since high school. He came over to say hi and we spoke briefly." "Did you happen to see if he picked up Steve's glass, you know, by accident or something?" "No, I was facing the other way when he sat down, so I wouldn't have seen him do that." "Did you happen to notice him slipping anything in Steve's drink?" "No. Like I said, we only spoke briefly and then he left." "OK, thanks Ronnie, you've been a big help," Bill said as he ended the phone conversation.

"Well, there's another dead-end," I said. Bill replied, "Let's hope Detective Petroskey has better luck. I'm beginning to feel less confident about our ability to prove that Scott is the murderer." "I'll call Sherry and give her the news that Detective Petroskey said that she should stop worrying about being a suspect," I said. Gillian is picking me up tomorrow. Will you keep me informed of any updates?" "Sure," said Bill.

CHAPTER 47

SHERRY'S RELIEF

Bill dropped me off at my hotel and I stopped in the restaurant for a bite to eat. When I got back to my room, I called Sherry and gave her the news. She was relieved that the police were no longer focusing on her as a suspect, but she was concerned about the poor prospects of proving that Scott killed Steve. "Will he get away with it, if the DA doesn't prosecute? That's crazy!" Sherry exclaimed. "Our justice system isn't perfect, but we still might find some incriminating evidence. We're not going to stop looking," I said. "Thank-you Connor for everything you and Bill have done for me. I don't know what I would have done without your help. I'm still trying to get over the shock of Steve's death, but at least I'm not facing jail, which was like a double punch in the gut," said Sherry.

CHAPTER 48

BACK TO NASHVILLE

Gillian picked me up the following morning and we discussed the case on the drive back to Nashville. Gillian said, "You're telling me that you're sure Scott is the murderer, but he might get off because you can't prove it." "Yes, as frustrating as that scenario seems to me, it may be the end result of this murder investigation. We have no DNA evidence, no eyewitness, and no clear video evidence that Scott dropped anything in Steve's glass," I replied. We sat in silence for a time contemplating the unfairness of the situation, especially to Sherry.

CHAPTER 49

KARMA

Two weeks went by, then four more weeks passed without any breakthrough in the case. Detective Petroskey couldn't make any headway with Scott's co-workers and Bill hadn't been able to discover any new evidence. However, the insurance company did finally pay Sherry.

Then yesterday I received a call from Detective Petrosky who said, "Connor, I'm sorry I haven't been able to make any progress on Steve's murder investigation, but yesterday it became moot. Scott Rossman was killed in a head-on collision with a drunk driver yesterday afternoon." I was stunned and unable to say anything for a minute. Finally, I said, "Does Sherry know this?" "No, I thought you might want to be the one to break the news to her," said Detective Petroskey. "Thank-you for letting me know and I'll call Sherry right away," I said.

After I hung up the phone, I just sat in my chair trying to comprehend what Detective Petroskey had just told me. When it finally sank in, I dialed Sherry's number. "Hello," said Sherry. "Hello Sherry, this is Connor. I've got some news about Steve's murder case. Detective

Petroskey just called me to inform me that Scott Rossman was killed in a head-on collision with a drunk driver yesterday afternoon." There was silence on the other end of the phone for a minute and I asked, "Sherry, are you still there?" "Yes," she said slowly. "It's just something I wasn't expecting." I said, "I know it's not the ending you wanted, but I hope it gives you some kind of closure. It's unfortunate that sometimes bad deeds go unpunished. But every so often, karma kicks in and levels the playing field."

EPILOGUE

Matt turned around and said, "Come on guys, we need to pick up the pace if we're going to make it to the top by lunchtime." A year had passed by quickly since our Crete adventures, and my track teammates seemed not to have changed much. We had decided to get together once a year for a new hiking adventure. Our plan today was to hike the five mile round trip from Cades Cove to Abram's Falls in the Smoky Mountains.

Bill, Henry, Donnie, Matt, John, Blake, and I had met yesterday in Knoxville for lunch at the Copper Cellar and reminisced about our fun adventures in Crete. After everyone had accounted for how they had spent the past year, we drove to Townsend, where we had hotel rooms reserved for the night. After an early breakfast this morning, we drove the sixteen miles to Cades Cove. We were dressed in our hiking gear and were ready to take in the pleasant smells and stunning fall foliage of the trail that meandered up the mountain beside the flowing stream. The sun was shining and the temperature was a brisk 50 degrees Fahrenheit on this October morning.

Matt was leading us up the soft leaf covered trail. Donnie said, "Wow, I like this soft footing better than our rocky paths in Crete."

Bill and Henry readily agreed. John and I were bringing up the rear. I had hiked this trail a number of times in my younger days, but Matt was leading our group because he had spent a lot of time on this and other nearby trails. His sister and brother-in-law had founded a very successful outdoor recreational company that developed hiking trails, bike trails, and zip lines in the area.

We picked up the pace and reached the falls by lunchtime. Bill and Henry picked out a large rock and sat down to retrieve their sandwiches from their backpacks. The rest of us followed suit. Donnie noticed two otters playing in the water and alerted us by saying, "Look at the otters." Henry quickly snapped a few photographs.

As we were eating, Bill asked me, "How is Sherry doing?" I responded, "Well, it's been a rough year, but I've kept in touch with her and she is doing much better now." John said, "I'm glad to hear that. I'm sure that her faith has helped her through her troubling times." Donnie said, "I saw her at the store a couple of weeks ago and she seemed to be doing OK."

We finished our lunch and began our more leisurely hike back down the trail. Our camaraderie was in full force again by the time we reached the end of the trail. We said our heartfelt goodbyes and promised to meet for another hike next year if our health allowed it. Our former track days had obviously played a part in keeping us in fairly good shape over the years. During our reunion hikes, our minds were telling us we were eighteen years old again, but the aches and pains in our 70 year old bodies were beginning to persuade us otherwise. We'll see how it goes next year.

THE END

www.ingramcontent.com/pod-product-compliance
Lightning Source LLC
Chambersburg PA
CBHW030824310726
48980CB00006B/630/J
* 9 7 9 8 9 9 2 9 9 0 2 0 1 *